Frozen Shadows

By
Gene O'Neill

JournalStone
San Francisco

JournalStone books may be ordered through booksellers or by contacting:

JournalStone
www.journalstone.com

ISBN: 978-1-942712-43-5 (sc)
ISBN: 978-1-942712-44-2 (ebook)

Library of Congress Control Number: 2015951509

Printed in the United States of America
JournalStone rev. date: September 11, 2015

Cover Design: Denise Daniel
Cover Art: Alan M. Clark

Edited By: Norman Rubenstein and Dr. Michael R. Collings

For Grams and Gramps

Frozen Shadows

Part I
Northern California

Mysterious Ailment In Mother Lode

A rare childhood disorder has reared its ugly head in Sutter Creek in the heart of Northern California gold country. In the last year, seven youngsters, ranging in age from eight to twelve, have been stricken down by a disorder that is mystifying local medical experts. The youngsters have been hospitalized at Sutter Amador Hospital in nearby Jackson, with symptoms that include severe headache/ anemia/malnutrition/ ongoing blood loss/low white blood cell counts. But the underlying cause(s) of these symptoms stubbornly elude hospital staff. A half-dozen specialists have been consulted and are also stumped as to the exact nature of the ailment. Several think it may be an exotic virus(s), which has not as yet been isolated by testing. A pediatric oncologist feels it could be a rare form of childhood leukemia, its specific cause(s) remaining undetermined. Local press directs attention to the possible carcinogenic conditions remaining at several gold mines now abandoned near Sutter Creek, where all seven youngsters lived and played. In any event, two of the children have reached the critical life-threatening stage.

—*The Sacramento Bee*, June 10, 1962

When I was six years old, I went to live with my grandparents in Sutter Creek. Shortly thereafter, I met a beautiful girl named Bell. Together, Bell and I would confront an evil man who cast no shadow. These three interrelated events would significantly influence the course of my life….

Chapter 1

June 1956

"You will love living in the country with them, Sean," I remembered my mother saying when she visited me that last Saturday before I left Children's Hospital in San Francisco. I had been there over six months, recovering from polio, which I had unfortunately contracted shortly before the Sabin vaccine became available.

"As soon as I'm on my feet financially, I will come and collect you," my single mother promised.

I never knew my father. He died—five months after I was born—in December of 1950 near the Chosin Reservoir in Korea, part of the famed General Chesty Puller-led 1st Marine Division breakout.

My father left the standard $10,000 military life-insurance policy and little else. Mother was a stay-at-home housewife, uneducated, with few outside job skills. With the insurance money stretched thinly and supplemented by Mom taking in other people's ironing, we barely struggled by for six years. Then I got sick and the medical bills began to pile up. The good news was that my mother had been offered an excellent opportunity to move in temporarily with her sister and brother-in-law in Sacramento and work full time at their rapidly growing family nursery—The Lone Oak Tree. She dearly loved gardening and tending plants. So Mom was upbeat and joyful that Saturday afternoon, enthusiastically telling me all about her new job in a new town.

"We'll be together as soon as I can afford our own place. And the future finally looks really bright for both of us, Sean." I didn't argue about me not going with her to live with Aunt El and Uncle Mike. She'd explained there was no room for me there, with three kids already falling out of beds in the small two-bedroom house.

But that Saturday visit was the last time I saw my mother alive. Returning to our small apartment on Louisiana Street in Vallejo, she was involved in a multi-vehicle accident, caused by a gas tanker jackknifing across lanes on Highway 40 and blowing up.

She never escaped her burning car, dying alone and young.

The following Tuesday morning, still burdened with grief, I was released from Children's Hospital and picked up by my grandfather, Thomas O'Donnell. He took me straight to All Souls Catholic Cemetery for my mother's memorial service. I'd had an almost miraculous physical recovery, no withered limbs or weakened lungs like many of my friends I was reluctantly leaving behind. So I easily managed the 100-yard climb uphill to Mother's graveside. After a blur of meaningless talk, mostly by people I didn't recognize, Gramps and I threw a handful of dirt onto her coffin and left. A disturbing, mind-numbing experience for a six-year-old boy.

My grandfather, a short, husky man, had a baritone voice made raspy from a life-long habit of smoking roll-your-own cigarettes, softened by his thick brogue. He took my hand in his gnarly, strong mitt, which he'd earned boxing as a youngster, working for Southern Pacific maintaining railroad track, and, for the last twenty-eight years, rigging at Mare Island Naval Shipyard in Vallejo. He'd retired four years ago from the Yard and moved to Sutter Creek to stretch his modest pension dollars. I didn't remember him from my early Vallejo years, and had seen him and Grams briefly on holidays twice or perhaps three times since their move. No Interstate 80 back then, and folks didn't make too many long car trips on the old two-lane, crowded State highways, except for maybe at Christmas or on Thanksgiving.

We left All Souls around eleven in the morning and rode nonstop from San Francisco into the Sierra Nevada foothills east of Sacramento for almost four hours before finally reaching Sutter Creek, getting barely acquainted on the way. I wasn't very talkative, still traumatized over my mother's untimely death and depressed by the formal, detached, routine nature of the burial; but I was successfully able to hold back any tears in front of this almost total stranger.

Chapter 2

Sutter Creek, backwater town on State Highway 49, had once played a significant part of Amador County's role in the famed California gold rush of 1849-50. A number of mine shafts had once surrounded the town, producing a substantial portion of the gold tonnage. Now the mines were closed, and fewer than 1000 people lived in the historic town. A few formed a solid core of established Anglo family names, some dating as far back as the 1850s; but a good number of them were "newcomers," many from immigrant stock, the majority of them Italians with a handful from Eastern Europe and Ireland.

Neither of my grandparents had lost their distinctive Irish brogues, even though they had arrived in this country as youngsters a decade after the turn of the 20th century. Both had only gone through the second grade in Ireland. After eventually settling in Southern California as an eleven-year-old boy, Gramps went almost immediately to work on the railroad, Grams came over five years later and finished the third grade here before quitting school to help her recently widowed mother and unmarried aunt in a small laundry on lower Tennessee Street in Vallejo. The laundry did fairly well, serving both the military and civilians from nearby Mare Island Naval Shipyard.

Apparently, my grandmother, Kathleen, was quite the redheaded, emerald-eyed beauty back in the day, with many avid beaus. But Gramps eventually claimed her hand. They married much later than most immigrants, because Gramps only quit the railroad down south and took a job in Vallejo at the Shipyard when he was at the advanced age of twenty-seven. One day soon after arrival in Vallejo he brought his laundry into the Erin Wash, and fell in love at first sight with the Gaelic beauty that waited on him. Grams said he didn't claim her twenty-three-year-old heart until after the first time they attended a dance—"Because that Donegal lad had grand feet blessed by St. Pádraig, his ownself."

The two worked hard and raised my father and his two sisters in Vallejo. Then after the three kids grew up and left home, Gramps retired early from the Yard at fifty-five, taking a reduced pension. By then he'd been involved in demanding, heavy labor for over forty years and had some recurring episodes of minor but painful back problems. He'd told Grams that he thought he'd maybe do light odd jobs around Sutter Creek if his general health held up. He was still robust and handy throughout his sixties and early seventies while I lived with them—an accomplished jack-of-all-trades, including farm and ranch work, with all the odd jobs he could handle.

I didn't have much family background on either of my grandparents before coming to Sutter Creek. And now, with their funny accents, they seemed exceedingly strange. Grams was quiet, rosy-cheeked, still freckled, and no-nonsense strict; Gramps was gruff-acting and smoked funny brown cigarettes he deftly rolled with one hand.

That first day I was nervous and unsettled arriving at their white and brown-trimmed, two-story wood-frame home on narrow Eureka Street, two blocks east of Main Street, next door to an old sand foundry. I was also feeling very sorry for myself, definitely missing my mother.

Of course, my grandparents had to have been a little unnerved, too, bringing a recently orphaned grandson they barely knew to a tiny, strange town off the beaten track to live with highly conservative people who looked, spoke, and acted differently from his mother and her working-poor friends in urban Vallejo.

But Gramps adjusted easily to the underlying tension. On the ride up, he'd managed to learn that I dearly loved books, even though my mother was not a book person and had not been able to afford many for me during the tough economic times after my father's death. Gramps shared my love of books and oral stories, too—no doubt a reflection of our shared Gaelic genes. His ongoing influence in appreciating literature and good writing would eventually have a dramatic impact on the arc of my life.

So, on my first late afternoon in Sutter Creek, after he showed me where to unpack and stow my tiny suitcase in my upstairs front bedroom, Gramps said: "C'mon, Sean boy, let's go downtown to a special place I think you are going to love."

We walked at a relaxed pace along Main Street—which was also State Highway 49—on old redwood plank sidewalks past a half-a-dozen businesses, Gramps reading signs aloud as we passed: Wells Fargo Bank, with its impressive, tall, black cast-iron doors; Marconi's Drugs, with its magazine and comic books in wide circular stands in front; The Chatterbox Café, with its breakfast and lunch daily specials neatly posted on a blackboard outside; Cabri's Food & Meat Market; Dom's Hardware & Dry Good's; Marie's Tailoring & Seamstress Work.

A narrow door leading to a darkened second floor was simply and mysteriously labeled "K.O.C." Gramps made no comment on these initials, but later I'd learn they stood for the Catholic fraternal organization: Knights of Columbus. The bulk of the Sutter Creek population was not Catholic, of course, attending either the First Baptist Church or Full Gospel Church in town or one of the several Pentecostal Churches in Jackson, the Amador County seat four miles away.

Finally, we stopped at the northern outskirts of town in front of what was once a small, but elegant, well-maintained, white and black-trimmed Victorian house. It was set back from the street-highway a good hundred-fifty feet, with a neatly lettered black-and-white sign in front announcing:

Amador County
Branch Library

Of course, I couldn't read the sign because I had missed much of my first year in school, even though I'd received a few lessons at Children's Hospital. And I probably wouldn't have known what a library was at that point anyhow. I don't recall Mom ever taking me to one in Vallejo.

In his wonderfully expressive Irish brogue—which I would soon learn to relish during nightly story-telling time—Gramps announced: "This is where all the right words finally come, Sean."

I looked at the small building, then frowned, and looked questioningly at my grandfather, wondering why the right words traveled here and how they even discovered this place?

He smiled thinly and continued in a nearly reverent tone: "Aye, lad, all the right words. When they have enough collected in there, they are carefully arranged into a group. Now, if they have selected wisely, and if they have put those right words in the proper order, something extraordinary and magical happens. They create one of God's true gifts...a wonderful book. Let's go in and inspect some of the magic."

We stepped into the tiny library, actually the entire bottom floor of the old Victorian, now mostly one large room with floor-to-ceiling rows of shelving that seemed to continue on and on forever.... All lined with books. Never had I seen so many books in one place. I was indeed awestruck by the marvelous sight!

"We can borrow these books," Gramps said, smiling at me.

After partially collecting myself, I said in a hoarse whisper: "But how many of these can I actually read, Gramps?"

He hesitated a moment. Then, in his engaging and heavily accented rasp he answered: "Oh, laddie, you can read them all...if you only take the time. Each and every one, to be sure."

He took my hand in his, led me to the desk to the right of the entry, and introduced me to Mrs. Sullivan. Cheerful-looking and slightly graying, the librarian made me a card and explained, with just the trace of her own brogue, the procedure for borrowing library books. With Gramps' help, I selected and checked out three children's books that afternoon. One was a thick, beautifully illustrated copy of *King Arthur and The Knights of the Round Table.* I treasured that book and eventually checked it out five more times in the next six months, before I finally received my own copy at Christmas—a beloved, well-worn book that I still own.

The Branch Library was indeed magical. I immediately fell in love with it, as Gramps had predicted, forgetting any worries while there that afternoon. During the ensuing years I would spend much of my spare time at the library—especially during the long, dark winters. It became a serene sanctuary, where I first experienced my tentative ambitions of a potential future life as a writer. Imagine, me, Sean O'Donnell. An aspiration that Gramps and Grams would eventually strongly encourage.

June 1958

With the help of Grams and Gramps, I quickly caught up in school during first grade. And by the summer after second grade, I was busy reading on my own, but also going fishing, bull-frogging, and helping on odd jobs with Gramps…and picking wild blackberries up the creek and fruit from the orchard out back with Grams. Later, on weekends in early September, I helped her can the surplus. But all that summer, reading at least two books every day.

In the evenings before an early bedtime, the three of us sat on the wide front porch, munching buttered popcorn and drinking lemonade or iced tea, flailing with opened hands at pesky mosquito dive-bombers. But Grams and I stayed and listened with relish, awed by Gramps' dramatic and wonderful Red Branch Tales about the exploits of the fearless hero, CuChulain, an Irish mythical/historical figure, who made the adventures of the Knights of the Round Table or the great Robin Hood's daring feats seem almost mundane.

He lived sometime in the First Century B.C. It was said he possessed the Gaelic heroes' mystical ability to place themselves into a trance-like state during combat, called *Riastradh* in Gaelic, later translated from ancient lore into English as "wasp spasm." The hero was figuratively stung and temporarily rendered calm, confidant, super-strong, absolutely fearless, and impervious to pain; it was at least strongly implied that the hero was also invincible. On several occasions I thought my Gramps might have been in the thrall of Riastradh; and much later, at two critical times, I think I was also able to invoke this state. At least at those moments I believed I was protected by the mystical trance. Gramps often smiled after recounting glorious Red Branch battle scenes, several times claiming we were in direct genetic lineage from CuChulain—perhaps not entirely in jest.

As a lad, CuChulain was called Setenta. He loved hurling, the national sport of Ireland, played a little like soccer but with a hurling stick and a hard ball—actually more of a cross between field hockey and lacrosse, but with no helmets or pads. One evening, when Setenta was twelve, he stayed outside his father's friend's stock compound to practice hurling. Unfortunately, the adults busy imbibing, talking, and laughing forgot that the young Setenta was outside and at dusk released the guard dogs—a pair of massive, aggressive hounds that circled the compound at night, protecting against surprise attacks by competing clans' stock raiders—the unofficial but real national sport of old Ireland.

The hounds attacked Setenta. A fatal mistake. The athletic, strong, mature lad, undoubtedly in a self-induced wasp spasm, caught each up by their hindlegs and swung them around his head, finally bashing their skulls together. Killed them both instantly on the spot. But under Brehon Law back then, if you damaged a person's property, you personally did whatever was necessary to make it good. Setenta took the guard dogs' place for a year, until two new hound pups were raised and thoroughly trained. By then he was known by his famous adult Gaelic name. His father's friend was called Culain. And *Cu* is "dog" or "hound" in Gaelic. Thereafter the lad was known as CuChulain—*Culain's Hound*.

Chapter 3

One afternoon early that summer of 1958, I was playing fetch with my little fox terrier, Snip, in the front yard, when someone shouted an order through the black, wrought-iron fence.

"Hey, you, Big Boy, come over here."

It was a girl about my age, maybe a bit older, but quite petite. She was standing with her hands on her hips, leaning slightly forward, wearing an aggressive, serious expression—a stance that I would soon learn was accompanied by a giant measure of better-not-mess-with-me attitude. But even then, at only eight years old, I recognized that she was already the most beautiful girl in town: curly blondish ringlets; faded-denim, twinkling eyes; and a constant hint of a smile that always looked on the verge of bursting into a raucous guffaw. A Swiss-Italian mixture of pixie princess and generous dollops of a rough-and-tumble, shenanigan-loving tomboy. How could I not be instantly smitten?

I sauntered to the fence, more than a bit curious but also intimidated by this intriguing girl.

She said: "I'm new in town, and my name is Isabella. Isabella Marconi. My dad is the new dentist here in Sutter Creek and over in Jackson, too. My Uncle Dominick runs the pharmacy downtown."

And is partners in half the other businesses along Main Street, too, I thought, but kept a sarcastic chuckle to myself.

"What's your name, Big Boy?"

I cleared my throat and answered: "Sean O'Donnell." Then I pointed at the house behind me. "My Gramps and Grams live here."

"Where do your parents live?" she asked, eyebrows arched.

"Gramps and Grams are my parents."

"You go to Sutter Creek Elementary School?" she asked, taking my curt response in stride with a slightly dismissive nod and frown, and continuing her interrogation.

"Yes," I said, feeling a little unsettled by this loud and confidently aggressive, but so tiny, girl.

"What grade?"

"Going into the third."

"How old are you?"

"I'm eight…but close to nine," I answered, stretching up as tall as possible and trying to puff out my skinny chest.

"I'm already nine, had a birthday weeks ago," she declared in a flippant voice, while looking me over carefully, before apparently resigning herself to an important decision. She even nodded to herself, confirming her judgment—a physical trait I would learn to pay close attention to over the years.

"Put your face right here," she ordered, pointing at a specific spot on the fence.

I complied, sticking my head between the iron stakes.

Without a trace of hesitation or the slightest blush, she put her hands behind my ears, roughly pulled me closer, and kissed me fully on the lips.

"You're now my boyfriend, Sean O'Donnell," she announced in a tone that left no room for argument. She stared sternly at me for a moment, daring any negative response, then added: "And you may call me, Bell…not Isabella or Bella or anything else girlish like that. Just Bell, do you understand?"

I nodded, still too dumbfounded to argue. It was the first time any girl had kissed me on the lips. Bell Marconi was not just any girl, either; she was a force of nature.

She smiled sweetly, recognizing my acceptance of her declaration. Then she dashed off, leaving me partially out of breath, standing with my hands dangling limply at the sides of my bib overalls but congratulating myself at having survived Bell's direct frontal assault.

I was officially designated Bell's boyfriend, and would remain in that favored capacity for as long as I lived in Sutter Creek.

A tiny town like Sutter Creek was somewhat like a '70s hippy commune, everyone minding everyone else's business. It was expected that all adults watched over all the kids, no one thinking twice about disciplining an errant youngster with a resounding swat on the pants—related or not. So everyone in town soon knew the adventuresome, charismatic, and feisty pixie; and not long after, they all expected to see us constantly together.

It wasn't a one-way or unrewarding relationship with Bell, either. No, indeed.

When the new comics—everyone called them funny books back then—came in at the pharmacy, Bell snagged copies of my favorites after the bundles were first cut open, before they were placed for sale on the stands, including issues of the purple-clad Phantom, the Blackhawk squadron, and, always my preferred first read, Plastic Man. During hot summer afternoons when we weren't swimming, playing ball, picking blackberries, wandering about, or doing some kind of chore, we read those funny books cover-to-cover at her Uncle Dom's drugstore fountain. We sat on high-backed round stools and sipped from frosty mugs of old-fashioned root beer—not poured from bottles or cans but made from scratch at the fountain by mixing syrup and soda water. Only two of the many fringe benefits of being Isabella Marconi's boyfriend. Another benefit of vital importance would be access to an unusual piece of equipment that would come in handy at the end of summer about four years later, an item that saved both our lives.

August, 1958

About two months after I'd kissed Bell and become her forever boyfriend, I met another new arrival in town, a remarkable third-grade boy who would quickly become my best guy pal, one of the kindest, gentlest souls I would ever meet, with a world-class sense of humor. At that time though, Bobby Mericalli immediately impressed me with his array of card tricks and a small collection of magic illusions that he'd brought to Sutter Creek from Wisconsin.

He was already a pretty clever magician. But as Bell saw it, he required a good Stage Director and PR Chief to showcase his skills. So late that summer and during the following school year, we presented four or five magic shows on the Central Park stage downtown, inviting all our friends. In addition, Bell spread fliers all over town before each performance, including prominent displays in each of her uncle's storefront windows. We charged a dime admission, too, which Bell diligently collected from everyone, no exceptions, including curious parents—this at a time when it only cost twelve cents to go to a double-feature movie over in Jackson. Of course I tagged Bobby with his theatrical name, the first time I introduced his act, and it would stick as his everyday nickname for the remaining four years of his very short life: Miracle Bob.

Bell, Miracle Bob, and I were inseparable for the next two years: magic shows, skinny dipping in a deep pool up the creek, constructing our own puppet plays with home-made puppets and colorful costumes, deftly climbing tall trees and steep cliffs, playing around the mine tailings, tossing a baseball or football, shooting baskets, visiting the library, and engaging in generally harmless shenanigans. Folks jokingly called us "The Miniature Three Musketeers," a name that of course delighted us. Actually, we were living a pretty charmed childhood...

Until Mr. Shadrach Black came to Sutter Creek and began to spread his cloud of ominous dark magic and misery.

June 1960

The town's namesake, Sutter Creek, flowed east and west about a hundred yards south of my grandparents' house, running parallel with Eureka Street and through the center of town, under the Main Street Bridge. By the end of summer, Sutter Creek had shrunk to little more than five or six inches deep, the snow-melt from the Sierras just a steady trickle by then. Nevertheless, that little stream supported a huge population of giant bullfrogs, each night a male chorus bellowing out its amorous charms.

Gramps taught me to snag them around dusk with a piece of red felt on a hook. I kept them in a wet gunnysack and sold them alive to my Italian lady customers around town for twenty-five cents apiece.

Chapter 4

Early that summer, an out-of-towner moved into the dilapidated, two-story Queen Anne—the old Rossi Place, as it was known—directly across the street from us, facing our way but on the other side of Sutter Creek. You accessed the house and four other old places on that side of the creek by a narrow public footbridge. But you could only see the second story of the old Rossi Place from street level or the footbridge, because willows and cottonwoods had grown up and screened it. If I looked over the trees from my second-story bedroom window, I could see the façade of the house and its huge front yard gently sloping almost to the creek and trees.

The new owner of the old Rossi Place appeared at our front door one day when Gramps was away for the afternoon, helping to gather grapes to test for sugar content at the Esposito Vineyards, ten miles in the country. Grams answered the knock at the door. And there stood a tall, thin, stooped man, with the bushiest eyebrows and blackest eyes I'd ever seen. Although it was a hot summer day, he was bundled in a loose-fitting dark blue duster over a long-sleeved, faded blue work shirt and cuffed dress pants. Unlike every other man or boy in town, who all wore boots or work shoes, this stranger sported a pair of highly polished black wingtips. He didn't appear to be anywhere near retirement age, like so many of the other recent arrivals to Sutter Creek—only late thirties, early forties at most. But those dark eyes, they were absolutely ancient.

"Hello, ma'am," he said, tipping his worn indigo driving cap politely to Grams. "I'm your new neighbor across the creek, Shadrach Black. I need some help moving a cord or so of fire wood to my new home." He pointed to a huge pile of cut oak that had been dumped on this side of the creek near the footbridge. "With your permission I'd like to hire your boy and perhaps one of his friends to help." He spoke with a slight foreign accent, but not Italian and certainly not Irish; and his dark figure standing there in his shiny dress shoes, with his spooky aged eyes, definitely gave me the shuddering creeps.

"Well, I think Sean would like that, to be sure." Grams turned to me. "Maybe your friend, Bobby, would like to earn some spare money, too?"

I reluctantly nodded to be polite. After clearing my throat, I said: "I'll go get him, Grams."

"Good enough," Mr. Black said. "See you boys in, say, about half an hour, down at the bridge?"

All afternoon, Miracle Bob and I pushed a wheelbarrow loaded with eighteen-inch black- and live-oak logs across the footbridge. We shuttled the heavy loads around back of the Queen Anne and dumped them in Mr. Black's unlit, gloomy basement, which was full of sticky spiderwebs. Then, as instructed, we stacked the logs neatly along a rickety stairwell that led to the first-floor kitchen. There were no locks on either the basement door or the kitchen door at the top of the stairwell—not unusual at all, not really needed in Sutter Creek back then.

We worked and sweated in 90-plus-degree heat all afternoon. Twice, we took a short breakn and made our way up the kitchen steps, to knock and request glasses of water from Mr. Black, who shared none of the heavy labor himself. Both times it took a long while for him to appear; and when he eventually did open the kitchen door, he seemed put out by our taking a break, the intrusion on his privacy, and our extravagant requests for water. He didn't invite us into the house; instead, he made us stand on the basement steps while he watched us drink. Then, he impatiently shooed us back to work.

At the end of the afternoon, after the last load was finally stacked, Mr. Black met us outside his basement door. He shook his head sadly, and, with a deep frown, announced: "You young *gadjos* are actually too lazy, much too slow, and you took way too many unnecessary breaks...But, here's your pay anyhow." Reluctantly, he thrust a shiny silver quarter into each of our hands as if he were parting with a treasured twenty-dollar gold piece.

Worn out, we staggered across the footbridge in a state of stunned speechlessness. Looking at the quarters in our hands, we couldn't believe what had happened. We had really been taken advantage of by this strange man. Even back in 1960, when the minimum hourly wage for a grown man was only around $1.25 an hour, one quarter for a full afternoon's labor by a boy was exceptionally stingy.

Miracle Bob was initially quite upset.

"I'm going to tell my Pops on the old skinflint right now," he said, taking off in a huff on his bike, pedaling toward downtown.

He lived on the other side of town, at the top of the long hill that ran past Amador High School—home of The Thundering Herd, arch-rivals of the Jackson Tigers. Along with Bell, we often played football on the field near the hilltop, we boys planning to star someday for The Herd. But I knew that even on his bike, Miracle Bob would lollygag on the pull up that long, steep hill, probably stopping when he reached the high school, especially if he saw someone playing ball on the field; and his genial nature would kick back in before he finally arrived home. Undoubtedly, he'd forget about informing his Pops about Mr. Black's tightfisted ways.

But I wasn't about to forget.

Fighting back tears later that evening, I showed Gramps the miserly single quarter I'd earned for an entire afternoon's work and blurted out my complaints against our cheap neighbor. "And in addition, he called us some kind of bad name too, Gramps. *Gadjos*, I think that's what he said."

He nodded, rubbed his chin, thinking for a moment, and then said in an even voice: "Okay, please sit down, Sean." I sat on the black leather ottoman by his matching recliner.

"A pair of good lessons to be learned here today, to be sure, lad. First, if you accept a job for pay, you always determine payment in advance. Either one total figure for the completed job, or an hourly rate. And second, you always value your own labor according to the danger or difficulty of the work and charge accordingly. If you don't charge enough, no one will care." He paused, smiled wryly, and added: "Long ago I discovered, if you work for nothing, you never have trouble finding work." He stared quietly at me for a moment, until I nodded my understanding. "Okay, good on you, lad," he said.

Then, he stood up, patted my shoulder, walked over and stopped by the kitchen door. He began to speak in Gaelic to Grams, but quickly caught himself, stopped, and switched to English. I'd asked to learn Gaelic when I first came to Sutter Creek and heard them speaking it. But Gramps had vigorously shaken his head and explained: "You look like them and if you speak like them, they don't know you are not one of them." He'd shaken his head again kind of sadly. "Grams and I will never be able to speak exactly like them. With that and our even casual practice of Catholicism, we will always be seen as different. Never truly belong here. But you already speak exactly like them. No Gaelic for you, lad. If you stay away from church, you have the perfect disguise." And that was sadly the last discussion with either of them about learning Gaelic. Something I would deeply regret later in life.

Leaning against the kitchen door-jamb, he'd switched to English and was saying, "Kathleen, I best be going over and meeting our new neighbor, Mr. Black. I believe he's a Brit or maybe even an Irish Traveler, perhaps speaking a bit of the Gammon to the boyos. I need to welcome him kindly to the neighborhood. Perhaps discuss a few things, like the local paying customs for half-a-day's work."

I would learn from Grams that a *Traveler* was called a Tinker when she was a young lass in Donegal. An Irish or Brit Gypsy. *Gammon* was a kind of Traveler secret language. And *Gadjos* was actually old Romany and meant non-Gypsy, but was often used in a derisive, dismissive, or demeaning manner. Grams warned that some Travelers were able to cast black magic spells and curses, which really intrigued Miracle Bob when I relayed that information. It didn't seem to frighten him at all. That boy was never spooked easily.

Despite Mr. Black being a tall, mysterious, and scary character, I knew that I wouldn't care to be in his shoes right now. My grandfather never seemed to show anger. But twice I saw him, perhaps, slip into a state of Riastradh during discussions with shrewd but ill-advised neighbors who'd contracted his services on odd jobs and afterward tried to chisel him on the fee. Both times my grandfather had cut the arguments short when he thrust out his square chin, a bright gleam in his eye. Not really red-faced and enraged, but calm, strong, fearless, and totally confident in the righteousness of his cause. Both neighbors used good judgment and readily settled up before any blood was shed.

Then, and again tonight, I pictured my grandfather as the avenging spirit of the old Irish mythical hero; and just like CuChulain going into battle, I imagined Gramps protected by a wasp spasm. Once, after I questioned him, he even told me how the heroes themselves invoked Riastradh. "They suck in a deep breath, hold it, close their eyes, and envision a tiny white-hot spot; and just like blowing up a balloon, they let out that breath and will that spot to grow. Then that expanding white-hot spot instantly flows across synapses, igniting the inner spirit, and warming the tips of all extremities," he said, with a wry smile. If he had his tongue in his cheek, I was too young to detect it.

Gramps returned shortly thereafter, meeting Grams and me in the dining room,where supper was ready on the table.

With a warm grin, he handed me a brand new five-dollar bill and said: "Mr. Black had a change of heart, Sean. He has decided that he underpaid you and your friend. Share that money with Bobby tomorrow, please."

"Thanks, Gramps!" I said, jumping up, taking the bill, and heading for the stairwell to the second floor to stash the money in my bedroom.

On the way up the stairs, I heard Gramps say to Grams: "Ah, Kathleen, I am believing our new neighbor is indeed a bit of a sharp trader, and more than likely a Traveler." He chuckled and added: "And I believe he cursed me with bad luck under his breath in Gammon when I took a little too vigorous of an exception with the measly amount he had paid the boyos. Probably figured I wouldn't have a clue to the meaning of: *Gajengi baxt*."

"Oh, is that right now?" Grams said, sounding more than just a bit ruffled with concern over the curse. "Well, we best be keeping our lad away from that man, no question. And you best not be getting mixed up with him, your ownself, Mr. Thomas O'Donnell." When she used the formal "Mr. Thomas O'Donnell," Gramps knew Grams meant what she said. The only heavier underlining of her intent was when she used his entire name with no mister: "Thomas James O'Donnell." When she blurted that out, even I stopped what I was doing, sucked in a deep breath, and steeled myself to weather the on-coming, blistering verbal storm.

I continued up the stairs, as Gramps laughed and interjected something briefly in Gaelic that made Grams loosen up and reluctantly chuckle. They both exhibited what I thought of as a distinctively Irish trait when they were thoroughly amused at someone's silly or inappropriate antics—conscious or not. Never a publicly demeaning snicker or a derisive snort or a verbal put-down. No, instead they chuckled privately, usually hiding behind their hands or looking away, fully enjoying the moment while not embarrassing anyone.

Later that night, I asked my grandfather to explain about Travelers and Tinkers.

He told me a little about the Tinkers of his youth, who wandered about Ireland in colorful horse-drawn caravans, usually patching metal things like pots and pans and sharpening knives. But modern Travelers no longer provided any of those once-valued services. He said he thought that Black was indeed a common name for an Irish or Brit Traveler. He said that they were all related to the ancient Romany. And like European or Mideastern Gypsies, they had a reputation for being tight-fisted, shrewd traders, clever fortune-tellers, and even privy to the ancient Dark Arts. He said that all over Europe and the Mideast there were unverified rumors of them stealing Gadjo babies for use in their secret rituals.

"Best you and your friends steer way clear of Mr. Black, Sean," my grandfather said, the deeply creased expression on his face lending weight to his caution. "Do not accept any more work assignments from him, regardless of promised payment."

Chapter
5

Avoiding our neighbor was not much of a chore. He was rarely seen outside, if at all. He appeared occasionally in the early evenings, just before the town businesses closed each day, returning home with a purchase from either the druggist or the hardware store. Even more infrequently were brief daytime trips around noon, always heavily bundled-up in loose-fitting clothes despite the heat, when he visited the Roma Inn just a block toward town. He didn't go to mingle outside with the old Italian men who gathered there, smoking crooked, smelly cigars, drnking dark-red wine, and arguing loudly in Italian while playing Bocce on a dirt court. Mr. Black watched only long enough to finish a small glass of wine, and then returned home. The odd thing was that, day or evening, I never saw him returning home with a bag of groceries from Cabri's.

June 1961

Whenever Mr. Black crossed the footbridge, headed for the Roma Inn, my little dog, Snip, ran along the wrought-iron fence, howling like a Banshee. For some reason, Snip hated the Traveler. But the little dog wasn't always patrolling the front fence; sometimes he was preoccupied with protecting the homestead against invading frogs, toads, and other varmints in the two-acre garden and orchard in our back yard—Grams grew corn, tomatoes, onions, squash, plums, apricots, peaches, cherries, figs, and apples. Then, after noticing the missing sentinel, Mr. Black would sneak up to the front fence, pick up a stick, and maliciously drag it along the metal spikes—*rat-tat-tat-tat-tat*—driving the little dog crazy.

One afternoon, after several of these noisy harassments, Gramps suddenly appeared out on the porch. With a stern expression, Gramps shook his finger back and forth, warning the Traveler in a no-nonsense voice: "That would indeed be just about enough of that tormenting that poor dog, Mr. Black. Do you clearly understand me, sir?"

The tall, thin man just hurried by, not acknowledging Gramps' admonition and muttering something to himself under his breath. Perhaps another Traveler curse.

Later that July, Snip turned up missing.

Of course, Bell and Miracle Bob were absolutely convinced that Mr. Black was the prime dog-napping suspect and had done something terrible to Snip to get back at Gramps for disrespecting him in public. I'd taken delight in describing my grandfather's stern reprimand of the Traveler to them.

But Gramps patiently explained to us, "You cannot accuse someone of doing something bad just because you do not like them. You need proof of their misdeed. Mr. Black is probably completely innocent of wrongdoing in this case. In fact, 'tis rattlesnake season, a lot of them over there along the nearby creek hiding in the shade of the blackberries. Quite possibly Snip might have poked his nose where it did not belong. He has never had a good measure of dog sense, often sniffing carelessly around those berry vines despite the snakes."

Sure enough, a day later Snip staggered across the footbridge, his head swollen to the size of a ripe cantaloupe, appearing like he'd been snake-bit on the tip of his dry nose. He came home whining and wagging his stubby tail. Grams made a hot-flax poultice and wrapped the little dog's snout in it—a home cure rumored to be effective for a snake-bitten dog. But it did no good this time. Early that evening, Snip crawled onto my lap and, with a final whimper, died. I was heartbroken.

Even though I wasn't one-hundred percent convinced that Mr. Black was responsible for Snip's death, Bell, Miracle Bob, and I schemed up ways to get even with the Traveler. We decided to stalk him whenever he went downtown for his evening shopping or afternoon drink of wine, one of us always tailing a good distance back. We kept details in a spiral notebook. Getting a good idea of the exact times of his daily and evening routine coming and going, always noting the date, time, and store names on the shopping bags.

One afternoon, around noontime, as Miracle Bob and I were casually tossing a baseball back and forth, Bell came rushing up. Only partially catching her breath, she managed to blurt out: "Boys…boys, he has no shadow, you know… I'm telling you, Mr. Black has no shadow!"

Stunned by Bell's bizarre claim, we looked up the street, where the stoop-shouldered man was at that moment walking toward us. As he passed and turned toward the bridge, Bell whispered, almost too loudly: "See! See there what I said. No shadow!"

It was true, Mr. Black didn't cast a shadow….

After a moment, I looked at the ground around us as we stood in the direct sunlight. We didn't really have discernible shadows, either, not more than an inch or so of indistinct dark puddles around our feet. Then, I squinted, glancing up at the sun overhead. And finally I chuckled and shook my head.

"Bell, no one has a shadow when the sun is at its zenith, a little after noontime around this time of the year—"

Recovering, she placed her hands on her hips, stuck her chin out in her belligerent Bell way, and snapped: "He didn't have a shadow five or ten minutes ago either, when he was going to town, smarty pants."

I didn't challenge her, deciding that discretion was the better part of valor.

"Well, let's watch close for the next week," I finally suggested, after giving her a few minutes to settle down. "Catch him on his next daytime walk. Maybe set up a special trap. Delay him from continuing on home for an extra ten or fifteen minutes. Let the sun drop just a bit to a more revealing angle. Check him out for a shadow after that delay—"

"Or more likely his lack of one," Bell said, frowning, her eyebrows slightly arched in a challenging expression.

Chapter 6

Six days later, a few minutes after noon, Miracle Bob stopped Mr. Black in front of our house before he could cross the footbridge. Both stood with their backs toward the west and the slowly angling sun. Bell and I were on the front porch, watching and listening, paying close attention. At the moment, neither of them cast a shadow that we could see.

"Mr. Black, I have a good buy for you on this basket of delicious, fresh-picked blackberries," Miracle Bob announced loudly, pushing the basket of prime berries in front of the Traveler. "Only fifty cents."

Mr. Black shook his head with a look of disgust. "Don't need any more berries, boy, and you're even higher priced than those ones at Cabri's," he said, starting to turn toward the bridge.

"Wait!" Miracle Bob said, grabbing at the cuff of Mr. Black's long-sleeved shirt. "These are really the fattest, the ripest, the juiciest berries in all of Amador County, including those down at Cabri's! An excellent buy."

"Hah!" Mr. Black said, vigorously shaking his head, looking more than a bit annoyed at being detained. "They are not a good buy, boy."

With his hand still clutching Mr. Black's cuff, Miracle Bob said, "Okay, okay, I'll tell you what I'm going to do. I'll make you a special deal you can't possibly refuse." A young, resourceful used-car dealer-in-training down there on Eureka Street.

"A special deal, you say?"

"Yes…how about you take this full basket for just twenty-five cents. And if those aren't the sweetest, juiciest, most delicious blackberries you've ever eaten, I'll give you your quarter back tomorrow. No questions asked."

Mr. Black smiled thinly but humorlessly. We could almost see the shrewd-trader wheels turning in his head. Forget about ethical. An opportunity lost was an opportunity lost. His smile broadened, as if he were thinking, *These berries are going to be free*! He couldn't pass up the deal, even if he didn't like the berries.

"Okay, money back if I'm not totally satisfied, right?" he said, digging a quarter from his coin purse and holding it in front of our friend.

"Absolutely correct," Miracle Bob said, glancing to where we were spying from the porch. He grinned, obviously proud of his own cleverness. By then the sun had probably dropped a degree or more past the zenith.

Mr. Black handed over the quarter.

But Miracle Bob held on to the basket of plump berries.

"Let me run into Sean's house and get you a nice paper bag to carry those, Mr. Black. You wouldn't want to spill and lose or bruise any of them."

At that moment we could see a blob of shadow extending east maybe six inches from Miracle Bob's feet—

"No, boy, " the Traveler said, "I don't need a bag!" He jerked the basket of berries out of our friend's hand, spilling several on the ground before moving swiftly in the direction of the footbridge.

"Okay, but don't forget these," Miracle Bob said, gathering up the three or four from the ground and trying to stall the Traveler for another few seconds.

But the stoop-shouldered man ignored him and strode away.

I glanced at my watch: 12:21. Both should be casting an observable shadow by now.

When I looked up, I could see that indeed Miracle Bob's shadow puddle was thinning, lengthening, taking on the rough form of a figure. By then, Mr. Black was in the shade of the oaks lining the walkway by the bridge. Yet for a micro-second before he reached the shade, the bundled-up Traveler was fully exposed to angled, direct sunlight....

I don't think he cast any shadow, but I wasn't sure.

I glanced at Bell, lifted my eyebrows, and frowned.

"See, Sean, see, he had no shadow!" she said loudly, looking at me sternly and almost compelling my agreement by the one-hundred-percent confidence in her tone.

"Bell, sorry, but I'm just not certain what I actually saw," I said, shaking my head. "He ducked into the shade too quickly after he got away from Miracle Bob. I couldn't really tell if he had a shadow or not."

Bell's look changed to a deeply disappointed frown.

And that's where we finally left our experiment: Inconclusive, despite Bell's obvious silent objection.

The next day, Miracle Bob refused to refund Mr. Black's quarter when the Traveler confronted our friend and demanded his money back. He first threatened the boy, and then cursed him in his foreign tongue. We didn't witness any of this, but, with a smug look, Miracle Bob related it to us later that day up at the football field, and laughed, discounting the threat of the Traveler's curses. He said he figured that he owed the skinflint some pay-back over the hauled firewood. Our pal was really much braver than me, no question.

To Bell's and my surprise, nothing happened to our friend as that summer wound down. Except for Miracle Bob getting a really bad case of poison oak all over his hands, arms, face, and eyes, which almost swelled completely shut for a couple of days. Slathered in pink calamine lotion for the next five or six days, the itchy, flakey, red splotches finally dried up. If that were the extent of the Traveler's curse, Miracle Bob indeed got off with relatively minor discomfort. And the three of us soon forgot about Mr. Black's lack of a shadow or the possible harm of his having placed a Traveler curse on Miracle Bob. Because other, more important things were changing as summer came to an end and the new school year began.

September-December, 1961

Bell, who was a couple of months older than Miracle Bob and me, had celebrated her twelfth birthday just before the beginning of summer vacation. And even before school was out, she abruptly quit going skinny-dipping with us on weekends at our pond up Sutter Creek. She was changing physically, with noticeable, intriguing bumps growing on her chest.

But I noticed other, less physical signs of change. She avoided all activities that could result in scrapes, bruises or excess dirt; and our once-adventuresome fearless leader was no longer interested in playing football or roughhousing. A sad state of affairs, we mystified boys agreed. But, of course, Miracle Bob and me were beginning to change a bit ourselves, too. My normally high-pitched, squeaky voice occasionally plunged deeper in tone at inconvenient moments—like during the announcement of Miracle Bob's magic final illusion, The Disappearing Dollar Bill, at a welcome-back-to-school performance.

Several months later, just before Christmas vacation, some of the older guys in our sixth-grade class were also changing noticeably in appearance and demonstrating some really curious weirdness, too, at least in their behavior toward the girls. Paying them more attention now, by harassing, teasing, and taunting them.

Through all of these confounding adolescent changes, I remained Bell's boyfriend; and she was stubbornly doing her best trying to teach me and Miracle Bob to dance The Twist and The Pony. An almost hopeless endeavor.

Chapter 7

May, 1962

The day before Memorial Day, Miracle Bob came down suddenly ill with some really bizarre symptoms: a terrible, unshakeable headache; extreme fatigue; run-down appearance, almost overnight; and, most worrisome to his family doctor, signs of sporadic internal bleeding. He had to be immediately placed in the ICU, alongside four younger kids from Sutter Creek sharing his symptoms, who had been hospitalized over the last six or seven months. Amador County Health authorities were beginning to worry about some exotic but as yet unidentified childhood epidemic sweeping the town. Maybe a new virus.

This scared me because of my devastating experience almost seven years earlier during the frightening polio epidemic in Vallejo, eventually determined to be viral. Everyone in town seemed to be growing tense about the mysterious ailment; the weekly newspaper covered it on the front page and helped stir up already anxious, apprehensive parents. Several editorials specifically focused blame on the potentially carcinogenic pollution at the abandoned gold mines. Lots of town kids explored around the old mines, sometimes playing on the steep tailings, including the three of us occasionally racing down on cardboard strips like sleds on a snowy hill, getting filthy dirty in the process.

Of course, during this unsettling and tense time, no one related this to Mr. Shadrach Black....

A week or so after Miracle Bob got sick, little Frankie Izzo came down with the same mysterious disease. Interestingly, he was actually able to talk lucidly and swore to his dad that Mr. Black had "stolen his shadow" and that's what made Frankie get sick!

Of course, the health and law authorities dismissed this as the delusional ranting of a severely ill youngster. But Miracle Bob, despite being almost too ill to speak coherently, whispered clearly to me during a short visit: "Frankie Izzo's right, Sean, it was him…the Traveler did it to me."

I didn't have time to question my friend further. And shortly after that all visits to the ICU were restricted to family members. It was the last time I saw my best friend alive.

Then, the day before school ended that first week in June, Bell, agitated and obviously badly worried, described to me what she had seen just before her eight-year-old sister, Lettie, was hospitalized with the same symptoms as Miracle Bob and Frankie.

Earlier that afternoon, Bell had been waiting for her sister to return from a birthday party at a classmate's home on the south side of Sutter Creek. From a distance, she saw Mr. Black spring out of the bushes behind Lettie and stomp on her shadow, stopping the young girl in place. He murmured a few foreign words, which Bell memorized; and finally Mr. Black reached down and ripped the shadow from Lettie's feet, as if it were a tangible, two-dimensional figure made from black pasteboard.

The shadowless youngster collapsed. Mr. Black hurried off, folding up the pasteboard shadow and slinging it over his shoulder as he headed toward the old Rossi Place. Bell had rushed across the footbridge and, with some effort, helped her dazed, confused sister onto her feet and walked her back to their home on the southern end of Main Street.

In a near comatose state, Lettie was transported to Amador Sutter Hospital in Jackson.

After hearing about that, I called an immediate meeting at our house that evening—Gramps, Grams, Bell, and myself.

Bell had told her father and uncle what she had seen. But they dismissed it out of hand, as one of Bell's "crazy fantasies," a product of her "hyperactive imagination." The two older men were even a bit angry because of Bell's insensitivity toward her little sister's serious illness. That's when Bell desperately turned to me for help.

Bell repeated her chilling story to the three of us. Grams and Gramps listened intently without interrupting until Bell stopped to catch her breath after finishing.

At that point, I said, "It's funny, Gramps, and maybe important, but Mr. Black might not cast a shadow himself. Last summer, after Snip died, we tracked him to the Roma Inn and watched him. We don't think he cast a shadow. But we weren't positive. With school starting and everything else going on, all the excitement, I totally forgot to mention it to you or Grams." I shrugged and made an apologetic face.

"Oh, and on my last visit to the hospital, Miracle Bob claimed that Mr. Black definitely caused his illness. He didn't say exactly how, though. And I haven't been allowed to visit him since then."

Unlike so many adults, who too easily dismissed unusual or fantastic claims by youngsters as being outlandish and incredible, my grandparents resonded differently. Some might say that, being born in rural Ireland, they were superstitious and believed in all kinds of fantastic and supernatural things—like leprechauns and banshees. But I like to think that at heart they were both tolerant and polite human beings, never discrediting another's beliefs or claims until actually disproved. Both were good listeners, even when children were talking. I always felt I could tell either of them anything.

Gramps nodded and said: "Okay. First, I believe you both. I vaguely remember as a lad hearing rumors about a man who cast no shadow, somewhere in Eastern Donegal, near County Tyrone. It was said the same man could conjure up evil spells, too. And I think there might have been reports some time later of an epidemic of rare children's disease along the Tyrone-Donegal border. I never connected all that at the time. And I can't recall anything about children losing their shadows or the eventual outcome of the mysterious disease.

"There were no TVs, phones, or even movies back then in rural, dirt-poor Ireland. Communication was direct, by mail, word of mouth, or just plain rumor at fairs. In fact, the tales of the man with no shadow died away quickly, and I do not think they were really ever mentioned again…."

His voice trailed off as he rubbed his chin thoughtfully.

After a moment he said: "Of course if what you say is accurate, and I do not doubt it, we cannot expect much help from the Sheriff over in Jackson or anyone else in authority. He may accept a complaint from me against Mr. Black, but when he reads the details, he will dismiss the complaint as coming from someone obviously unbalanced, crazy even. If we are to get to the bottom of this and keep Mr. Black from stealing any more shadows—and thereby prevent any more children from landing in the hospital—then I am afraid we must take matters into our own hands."

"Ah, you best be taking care now, bothering with this dangerous Tinker man," Grams warned. "Dealing with his devilish curses and all. Your ownself will be landing in the hospital or perhaps far worse, even ending up horizontal in the cemetery. I do not want to be conducting an Irish wake for you, do you hear me, Thomas James O'Donnell?"

Gramps patted her hand. But Grams jerked her hand away and gave him a stern look. "Did you be hearing me?"

"I did, of course."

"What should we do, Gramps? Do you have a plan?"

He nodded. "Aye, perhaps a beginning of one, anyhow," he said, while obviously thinking hard.

"I suspect we first need to determine why Mr. Black stole those shadows. What is he doing with the shadows he has claimed? And how might that relate to the sick children? We need to do some close surveillance. Watch him at all hours, if that is possible with our limited numbers."

He paused and again touched his chin.

"How can we do that, Gramps?"

"Well, we can begin by setting up watch headquarters on your bedroom porch, Sean. From there, we can easily observe Mr. Black's yard, front porch, all his front windows, and his comings and goings across the Sutter Creek footbridge—"

"Let's begin tonight!" Bell interrupted. "I'll get permission from my parents for a sleepover. Sean and I will take the first watch tonight, Mr. O'Donnell."

Gramps chuckled, recognizing what I already knew so well: Bell's can-do-right-now-take-no-prisoners-adventuresome spirit.

He said: "Okay, lass, that will be a grand start, to be sure. Let me think some more about our next step."

Our meeting broke up.

Later, Bell and I laid out our sleeping bags on the little porch outside my bedroom window. There was plenty of room for us to sit in them, side-by-side, propping our backs against the wall. It was exciting being so close to her and alone. But we were also watching the old Rossi Place….

We must have dozed off some time before midnight.

The next thing I knew, Bell was shaking me awake and pointing toward the old Rossi Place.

It was midnight and there was a full moon overhead, lighting up the front yard brighter than day.

Mr. Black was in full view, standing there completely naked, in the middle of a kind of circle that resembled a clock face with some black lines radiating from him. On closer inspection, I could see that they were not thin lines, like on a timepiece, but two-dimensional supine figures, and I counted not twelve but only seven.

"They're the missing shadows, Sean!" Bell whispered. "They have to be the shadows stolen from the seven kids at the hospital! He's conducting some kind of weird mystical ritual with them, under the full moon. We may be looking at the explanation for this recent rash of hospitalizations. It's not a virus or bug or leukemia at all. It's the Traveler's Black Magic—!"

"I'm waking Gramps," I interrupted, and slipped inside the house, hustling down the hallway to my grandparents' bedroom.

Despite the hour, Gramps got right up and followed me back onto the little porch.

The three of us stood there, fascinated by a Dark Arts Rite being conducted under the light of a bright silvery moon. We couldn't tear our eyes away.

Naked, Mr. Black stood in the center of the circle, the seven supine two-dimensional figures lying still. He slowly made his way around the perimeter of the circle, bending over and gently tapping each figure three times on its head, while issuing forth a foreign incantation.

Returning to the center of the circle, Mr. Black lifted his hands like a puppet master. And the shadows rose to their feet, standing in place, as if resurrected.

More elaborate hand movements followed. But nothing really happened for a few long moments.

Then, as if they'd all been simultaneously plugged-in, the two-dimensional figures shuffled stiffly forward like zombies, slowly reducing the perimeter of the circle, until they touched the nude Traveler and clasped hands around him.

For maybe a half a minute, the dark figures stood perfectly still, as Mr. Black chanted more, while gradually straightening, growing a little taller, and even filling out a bit. Momentarily, he glanced our way, and his dark features appeared youthful, sexually excited, as he peered up and grinned evilly at the glowing moon.

I felt chilled by that nasty leer.

A few moments later, the ritual apparently concluded, Mr. Black effortlessly gathered up and draped the limp, lifeless shadows across his right shoulder. It was as if they'd been drained of not only weight but of spirit—their very *élan vital*. He made his way onto his front porch. Just before he disappeared into the house, we were all astonished to see that in the glistening moonlight, Mr. Black definitely cast a long shadow across his wide front porch.

At that revealing moment, the naked Traveler disappeared inside the darkened house.

"What happened, Gramps?" I asked in a hoarse, puzzled voice.

"I'm not completely sure, lad," he answered, rubbing his chin. "But no question that Mr. Black is using those shadows he stole for his own devilish purposes. Perhaps draining the youthful essence of their owners into himself. This is undoubtedly linked to why the shadows' owners remain so sick and are getting worse by the day."

He nodded and added: "Maybe Mr. Black is much older than he seems, maybe even primordial. And perhaps he's an ancient demon…possibly summoned up by the Tinker and now possessing him."

Which confirmed what I had felt when I looked into the Traveler's ancient eyes the day we met. It was like staring into the distant past.

"Well, what do we do now, Mr. O'Donnell?" Bell asked, hands on hips, not appearing fazed by this mystifying, and to me, terribly frightening strangeness.

Gramps thought a few moments, then said: "Well, I think we need to rescue and free those shadows. And the sooner, the better. We cannot leave them in the Tinker's—or the Demon's—control, continuing to drain the very life from those poor sick children. Perhaps, at the same time, we can figure out some way to capture Mr. Black's shadow—"

"But he doesn't cast a shadow during daylight, Gramps," I said. "Maybe only, like just now, a special one cast at midnight in the full moonlight."

Gramps nodded thoughtfully.

"Okay, here's what we are going to do tomorrow, if the Tinker leaves to walk downtown…."

Bell and I would enter the old Rossi Place through the basement when Mr. Black was gone and search downstairs and upstairs, if necessary, to locate the missing shadows. Gramps would stand guard in the trees near the bridge and whistle to warn us when he saw the Traveler returning home. When we heard that, we were to scurry out of the back of the house to safety.

He clasped his hands and gave a distinctive loud, deep cooing sound, something like a California quail's warning call. Gramps suddenly stopped whistling and snapped his fingers.

He smiled and beckoned to Bell: "I have another grand idea, lass. Might just work, too. Maybe you can help obtain the special equipment we will need from your uncle's hardware store."

He asked me to help Grams make a little midnight snack—toasted-cheese-and-bacon sandwiches and lemonade—while he and Bell discussed a side project, pertaining to that secondary, but perhaps just as important, goal of capturing Mr. Black's shadow.

Chapter 8

We all met at 11:30 a.m., Bell carrying the special item in a small brown paper bag. Gramps looked inside, nodded, smiled broadly at her, and asked: "Batteries installed?"

She smiled, arched her eyebrows, and nodded, her expression suggesting, "Well, of course."

Gramps again outlined his plan for searching the old Rossi Place for the stolen shadows. We both repeated our assigned roles. Then Gramps showed me what was inside Bell's mysterious bag and gave us our additional assignment, which would be required after he used the special piece of equipment. The plan required fast and excellent timing on both our parts, after Gramps switched on the device.

Finally, he asked: "If this thing works as I hope, you two know exactly what to do, am I correct?"

I nodded.

"Yes, we do, Mr. O'Donnell," Bell said confidently. "We'll be watching for when you first flip it on."

We waited on our downstairs front porch.

We were in luck!

Around noon, I spotted Mr. Black outside, crossing our way on the footbridge. He turned and headed up Eureka Street toward the Roma Inn.

"Okay, both of you scoot over and search his place," Gramps said. Tucking the brown bag under his arm, he added, "I'll be in the trees by the bridge. Get out of there fast when you hear my whistle.

Bell and I entered the old Rossi Place through the unlocked basement, armed only with a pair of small plastic camp flashlights.

We looked around the basement for a minute or so, without spotting anything in the gloom, except to notice that Mr. Black had been using some of the wood Miracle Bob and I had stacked. Then we crept up the stairs to the unlocked kitchen door.

We found no refrigerator or cupboards inside the kitchen, only a huge wood-burning stove. A large blackened copper kettle atop the stove contained about a gallon of clean water. Whatever he boiled in the kettle, Mr. Black needed a lot of firewood. We continued on, scanning with our flashlights, finding the rest of the darkened first story completely devoid of furniture. The floor was covered with a thick layer of dust, with no trace of anyone living there…except for several sets of footprints leading to the stairs, probably all the Traveler's.

We climbed the stairwell and glanced into the four bedrooms, finding each also empty of furniture, the hardwood floors again dusty—

"Listen, Sean," Bell whispered.

I cocked my head.

"Hear that?"

I nodded.

Sure enough, above us I heard the steady hum of what sounded like…a small generator, like the one Gramps sometimes used on his projects.

We followed Mr. Black's footprints back to the fourth bedroom. With her beam, Bell tracked the prints to a corner ladder leading into an open crawlspace to the attic.

We climbed the ladder.

When I poked my head into the attic, the hum was much louder.

I shone my flashlight at the origin of the sound.

A small generator was hooked up to an extra-large air-conditioning or refrigeration unit next to a tiny square room in the center of the attic. The room was about six feet by six feet, and six-and-a-half feet high, constructed of heavy plywood scraps and two-by-fours, with no windows and one narrow door. Everything was roughly fitted together and amateurishly patched with duct tape, apparently sealing exposed seams. We crept past the generator and cooling unit and paused at the unlocked door.

Cautiously, I rested my hand on the door. It felt cold, like an icebox door.

Bell reached past me and pushed the door open—

A rush of icy air instantly engulfed us.

We shivered violently.

Bell shone her flashlight inside.

Then stepped in.

I followed.

She played the light over a cot at the center of the room—

Abruptly, she stopped.

Because there, in a neat row along the back wall, draped on coat hangers like thin black garments in a closet, were the seven shadows. Hanging stiff and lifeless.

Bell approached the tiniest shadow, stopped, and, obviously choked up, whispered hoarsely: "This has got to be my Lettie's…." She gently touched her sister's shadow but drew her hand back quickly, as if burned. "It's coated with ice and frozen stiff."

At that moment, I heard something downstairs…footsteps, sounding like they came from the basement.

We both stood still and listened intently.

Someone was down there…and noisily climbing the kitchen steps. If it was Mr. Black, why hadn't Gramps whistled and alerted us?

The kitchen door squealed open, and we held our breaths.

Nothing, not a sound for what seemed the longest time.

Then, before we could finally breathe easier, we heard loud footsteps again, climbing upstairs…and moving into the back bedroom right underneath the crawl space.

Quiet again.

Bell silently grasped my arm and pulled me into the chilled closet. We eased the door almost shut. If it was indeed Mr. Black, we could only hope he wasn't visiting his frozen shadow-prisoners. Because if he was, we were trapped. Not good, not good at all, I thought, resisting a shiver.

My heart was thumping, my pulse racing as if I'd just run a four-minute mile. Next to me, Bell shuddered. I too clutched her hand in mine, squeezing it tightly, leaned close, and forced a smile. She nodded.

Minutes slowly crept by....

Nothing happened.

Maybe the Traveler wasn't coming up here after all. Could we be so lucky?

I began to release a breath held much too long....

A voice shattered the silence, driving an icicle deep into my chest and chilling me even more than the icebox: "I've followed your footsteps through the house to the attic. I know you are in that freezer, Gadjos."

No question...it was Mr. Black's voice. And he knew we were hiding in the icebox with the frozen shadows. He'd gotten past Gramps, but we didn't have time to wonder how that had happened.

I was having real trouble breathing now. Scared shitless.

But we both knew we had to suck it up, fight, and hope that Gramps or someone would come to our rescue. I took some comfort in gripping my plastic flashlight—a short club, but better than nothing.

Glancing at Bell, I motioned for us to separate. We moved to either side of the narrow door, preparing to assault Mr. Black from two directions. Maybe we'd be lucky.

"Come out, right now," he ordered.

I vigorously shook my head, sucked in another deep breath, and steeled myself. My eyes had adjusted to the darkness, so I could see that Bell had her serious game face on, too. We weren't giving up. No way. The Traveler was in for a fight. I squeezed my eyes closed, and there in my mind's eye was the image of a tiny white-hot dot. I breathed out; the dot expanded. And as the heat from the expanding dot engulfed my body, I felt a calm settling over me, a strength surging into my extremities, and my fear dissipated like fog on a sunny morning.

Wasp stung!

"I'm coming in to get you," he said—his threatening tone should have been absolutely terrifying. I ignored it.

The attic floor creaked loudly.

He was coming for us.

I bent at the knees, ready to deliver a powerful blow, my heart rate and pulse under control now. Bell had lifted her flashlight high over her head with both hands, as if it were an axe. We were prepared to defend ourselves as much as possible—

The door was flung open, and a bright light shone past us toward the back wall and the seven frozen shadows.

Even though it wasn't shining in my eyes, I was still partially blinded.

But at that moment we heard a wonderful, rich baritone with a thick brogue, coming from near the crawl space. "Hold it right there, Mister," Gramps shouted from behind Mr. Black. And I was convinced that he too was enthralled in a state of Riastradh.

The light instantly flashed away as the Traveler turned…to face Gramps, who was pushing through the crawl space.

With a few supernaturally quick steps the Traveler was halfway back across the attic floor, menacing, headed toward my grandfather.

But Gramps had already taken a huge, handheld floodlight from his brown bag and flipped it on, as planned.

"I said *stop*!"

The tightly focused beam totally engulfed Mr. Black like an intense stage spotlight and stopped him in his tracks.

And his long, thin shadow suddenly stretched across the attic floor to within a few inches of where Bell and I stood in the wide-open doorway into the icebox.

Gramps had been right! Mr. Black cast a shadow when caught in intense artificial light. Now it was up to the two us.

Without hesitating, and as previously instructed by Gramps, Bell jumped and pinned the Traveler's shadow to the attic floor with both feet, keeping Mr. Black in place. Quick-witted Bell had memorized the magical words when her sister's shadow was taken; and last night she'd carefully sounded them all out to Gramps: *"Gajengi…baxt…genta…resi."*

He repeated the spell.

After the last word, I moved, per Gramps' explicit instructions, and stepped several steps closer to Mr. Black; then, bending over, I gripped the Traveler's shadow in both hands, and, with my trance-induced super-strength, tore it from his feet.

It made a loud ripping sound, and at that, all movement in the attic seemed suspended: Everyone frozen in space and time…

Then, a minute later, light burst from where the Traveler stood, as if he'd exploded from within, illuminating the attic and momentarily blinding the three of us.

I rubbed my teary eyes, blinked several times, and took a deep breath…finding myself released from the grip of the wasp spasm.

Mr. Black wasn't there any longer.

He couldn't have possibly gotten past Gramps, who was still near the crawlspace, holding the strong floodlight.

Questions swirled in my head:

Had he been blown to pieces?

Was he truly neutralized?

Or had he somehow escaped?

If so, where had he gone?

Or…what?

There were no answers to any of these questions.

One moment Mr. Black was standing there in the attic, and the next he was not; the mysterious Traveler—or Demon or whatever he was—had vanished, leaving behind absolutely no trace.

Bell summarized it best at that moment, whispering: "Thank God, the Genie is back in the bottle!"

Gramps came to us and asked, "Are you both okay?"

I nodded.

And Bell said: "Yes, we're fine, Mr. O'Donnell."

"I'm sorry, I was unable to warn you. The Tinker spotted me before I could manage my whistle, even stopped a moment and peered at me, probably wondering why I was lurking in the trees on his side of the footbridge. He kept glancing back at me, so I was afraid of alerting him to your presence in the house by whistling. But I followed as soon as possible the moment he disappeared into the basement."

Bell nodded. "Don't worry, it turned out okay, Mr. O'Donnell. You came to our rescue in time. I'm just a little frightened still."

I was too dumbfounded over actually experiencing the thrall of Riastradh and the Traveler's subsequent disappearance to say much of anything. So, I just stood there, thankful we were all in one piece. Trying to catch my breath and gather myself.

Chapter
9

After we partially regained our composure, we squeezed past the cot in the icebox, collected the children's frozen shadows, and carried them downstairs and into the warm night. Bell and I sucked in several more deep breaths, trying to quiet our badly shaking hands. It was a miracle we'd been able to keep it together long enough to perform our vital roles in capturing Mr. Black's shadow. I thanked my Gaelic genes and Gramps' instructions for the enabling power of the wasp spasm—not caring if it had been imaginary or not.

Noticing our trembling hands, Gramps smiled and said: "Ah, lad and lassie, you were both sterling. A pair of heroic giants. CuChulain his ownself would have been proud of you, 'tis true." And then he winked at me, and nodded knowingly, as if we were indeed fellow conspirators in a secret spell.

Beaming from the praise, we carried the icy shadows home and draped them over the front porch railing to thaw. I counted seven. Mr. Black's long, tall shadow was not among the rescued ones. We must have somehow missed it, left it behind in the attic after the Traveler disappeared.

Grams was waiting with huge mugs of steaming hot chocolate that warmed and finished relaxing us. I was too exhausted to worry about Mr. Black's missing shadow, retaining only enough energy to sip the delicious hot drink.

Grams and Gramps chatted excitedly back and forth for a few moments in Gaelic. Then she smiled broadly, with obvious relief at his answers, and hugged each of us tightly, rubbing our backs. I felt much better after that.

Gramps made a few observations that hadn't occurred to Bell or me. "I'm guessing Mr. Black was boiling water downstairs in that big black kettle. Maybe using it to thaw the shadows before he performed his rituals outside and to coat them afterwards. The water would freeze to a thin layer of ice in the special room. And that cot... I don't think Mr. Black was lying up there guarding his victims. I think he may have also required the icy temperature himself. Certainly, he comes out in the daylight only at noon to cover his lack of shadow. But you notice he is always completely heavily bundled-up in loose clothing, like a desert Bedouin warding off the heat. I suspect he likes neither sunlight nor summer heat. Who knows, maybe direct contact with either might be damaging or possibly lethal to him."

Bell chuckled and said half-jokingly: "Like a vampire during the day in the movies, right, Mr. O'Donnell?"

Gramps nodded, smiled thinly, but didn't indicate full agreement with Bell's analogy.

The next morning the shadows had disappeared from the front porch! And an hour or so later—not surprisingly, I thought—we learned that five of the youngsters in the hospital were beginning to rally. Unfortunately, Miracle Bob and Lettie passed away from complete liver and kidney failure during the early evening.

Bell and I were sad...heartbroken...that we hadn't been able to rescue the shadows earlier and blast Mr. Black off to wherever he came from, perhaps freeing her sister's and Miracle Bob's spirits in time to save their lives....

But at last, the horror was over. Now plausible explanation needed to be spread through in the community to ease folks' minds. *The Sacramento Bee* took care of that.

Suspected Carrier Disappears

Medical authorities suspect that the seven youngsters recently hospitalized in Sutter Amador Hospital in Jackson were infected with a mysterious ailment, perhaps a super-bug, after coming in direct contact with Mr. Shadrach Black. The suspected pathogen, possibly an unidentified virus, caused similar symptoms in all the children, resulting in two deaths. Fortunately, the other five surviving youngsters are rapidly improving and will be released from the hospital next week. The suspected carrier of the disease, who lived in Sutter Creek, has disappeared. All efforts by local law enforcement and health authorities to contact Mr. Shadrach Black have failed. Mr. Black had lived locally for less than two years, and he seems to have been a virtual recluse, only venturing out in the evening or occasionally at noon time. He has no known local relatives or friends. He seems to have left no trail, paper or otherwise, after abruptly disappearing. Efforts to track him are under way, including law enforcement officials putting out an APB. Amador County health authorities hope ongoing efforts to contact the suspected carrier will soon be successful, so they can administer a battery of tests and perhaps get to the bottom of the medical mystery.

—*The Sacramento Bee,* June 15, 1962

October 10, 2012

Of course, that all happened over fifty years ago.

Grams and Gramps are long gone.

Smoking those old brown roll-your-owns finally caught up with Gramps big time—cancer of the esophagus. He died hard but fairly fast, a mere shell of himself, starving to death even with feeding tubes jammed down his throat. At the end he weighed less than ninety pounds, able to only suck on lime or lemon popsicles, which at one time he had dearly loved. His cancer diagnosis was confirmed shortly after I left Sutter Creek for my freshman year at Sacramento State University.

Grams had called just before Easter vacation, and I came home and spent almost the whole week with them. Luckily, I was able to say goodbye to the grand old man, tell him all the remarkable things that made him so special to me and why he'd live forever in my heart and memory—something most people unfortunately never get around to doing with their loved ones before they pass on. And I swear that an hour or so before the end, the frail old man was able to close his eyes, pull himself together, breath in deeply, and call on Riastradh, dying with all the presence, strength, grace, and calm dignity of a true Gaelic warrior.

Ten years after Gramps died, Grams came to live with us in Sacramento. She passed on naturally at eighty-five, cheerful and happy to the end, but perhaps slightly demented. These two wonderful Irish-Americans left me armed with a pair of splendid literary gifts: A life-long, deep love of books and a lasting strong drive to succeed with my own writing efforts.

Now, thanks to them and some sustained effort, I'm making a comfortable living as a full-time writer. My experience with the mysterious Mr. Shadrach Black way back then undoubtedly left a lasting imprint on my literary sensibilities, resulting in a lifetime obsessive interest in exploring through fiction the darker side of man and myth. After finishing the Clarion Workshop For Writers in 1979 at Michigan State, I've gone on to publish over a hundred and twenty short stories and novellas, and six dark-fantasy/horror novels. Two of those novels, a pair of novellas, and several short stories have been nominated—with the pair of novels winning—the coveted Bram Stoker Award®. I have had a deeply satisfying writing career. I only wished Gramps had lived to see the beginning of it.

Bell was crowned Miss Amador County while we were seniors at Amador High School, representing us that following summer in the Miss California contest. She didn't win, but a year later, she realized a dream and became a successful model, working for six-and-a-half years in Milan and New York City. After I graduated from college with a degree in English and Creative Writing, I proposed to Bell at the Rockefeller Center Skating rink, on a knee at center ice; and we were married soon thereafter in the Big Apple, honeymooning in Italy.

But we returned to Sacramento to live, take care of Grams, and raise our two children. Bobby and Lettie are grown now, with families of their own, living in Oakland and San Diego. Both successful, although Bobby never showed much or his namesake's interest in magic. He's a social-services guy, working in a program that helps at-risk kids. He has one son, TJ. Lettie was a full-time cardio-vascular surgical Physician's Assistant before she started her family—twin girls, Kathleen and Fiona. So, now Bell and I have three wonderful grandchildren. We spend as much time with them as possible, even though we both continue to work and to travel quite a bit.

Bell and I have indeed been fortunate, leading almost a charmed life together, beginning with that first wonderful kiss through the wrought-iron fence, some fifty years ago....

Except that early this evening, I realized Bell had something important for me to see and hear, when she stuck her head into my study and disturbed my writing in this journal—breaking a normally rigidly enforced do-not-disturb-the-writer rule. She beckoned me follow her back into her studio, where she conducts a part-time but highly successful commercial graphic art design business. The State of California is one of her best customers.

She pointed at the screen of one of her three computers—to the frozen CNBC News.

She clicked the delay back on.

It was the middle of a report on a mysterious ailment affecting four McDowell County youngsters from the remote village of Upper Dry Fork, in a once prosperous coal-mining area of southwestern West Virginia. A doctor was reporting to a small group of concerned parents and townsfolk outside the courthouse in nearby Bradshaw, the county seat. The symptoms were all chillingly familiar, and hearing them repeated on TV raised the hackles on the back of my neck. The doctor thought the children might have contracted some new and as yet unidentified exotic disease, but the medical experts did not yet agree on the specific pathogen. There was a brief discussion from several in the audience of the possibility of contamination lingering around the nearby boarded-up coal mine shafts, and run-off from the mountain top strip-mines further to the northeast somehow having caused this, with maybe more cases coming to light.

Déjà vu…

"Here, this is what I especially wanted you to see," Bell interrupted, frowning, as the TV camera panned across the concerned and worried faces of the small bundled-up audience shivering in the brisk autumn air. Bell stopped the picture again. Then, she fiddled with one of her technical gizmos and blew up the captured image in the middle of the audience.

The picture was pretty dark and grainy.

But I easily recognized the man with the bushy eyebrows and ancient black eyes, who had miraculously not aged a bit in the last fifty years. He looked exactly the same as that day Grams first opened the door to him in Sutter Creek.

Bell murmured: "Sean, the Genie is back out of the bottle."

Chapter 10

"What are we going to do now?" I asked, stunned, realizing that the man who had cast no shadow in Sutter Creek was still alive and practicing his deadly black magic again. We hadn't sent him permanently to Hell from the attic of the Old Rossi Place. He'd survived.

"We should call someone in West Virginia right now," Bell said, taking out her cell phone and nodding. "The police department or county sheriff responsible for that area…or maybe the local health authorities would be better?"

I cut her off, shaking my head. "And tell them what, Bell? That we were present fifty years ago, when an ancient Traveler/Demon stole seven children's shadows in Sutter Creek, performed naked midnight rituals that caused symptoms in his victims similar to those the West Virginia children are suffering right now?" I smiled wryly and shook my head. "You know what…they'd just laugh. A smart one that didn't bother to hang up on you immediately might ask: *Why didn't you report this back then? Why did you keep this to yourselves all these years?* And your answer would be…?" I let my voice trail off dramatically and then shrugged.

She leaned forward, almost blurting out something, but only frowned and peered at me with arched eyebrows, her hands on hips. Almost the full-blown Bell look.

I restrained a chuckle, while thinking: *Well, they might not want to actually laugh in Bell's face if they know what's best for them. No, I didn't think that would be advisable.*

She thought another moment, then eased back on her heels, her features relaxing, and nodded, finally acknowledging that I made good sense.

Then, she announced: "Well, we will have to travel to that part of West Virginia ourselves and find Mr. Shadrach Black again, before he makes any more kids sick. Free those four shadows that he probably has frozen and stashed away somewhere. Get rid of him again. Just like we did way back in the day at Sutter Creek. And find a way to do it permanently this time."

"But we aren't those same energetic, lucky, naïve, twelve-year-old kids anymore, Bell. We've slowed down just a step or two, you know. We don't have Gramps' guidance and good judgment backing us up either." Raising my eyebrows, I hoped to get some agreement on these important points, too, from her.

But she stubbornly faced me, hands on her hips, resurrecting that old confrontational expression—the full-blown Bell attitude. And at that moment I swear I flashed back to that day I first met her, when I was only eight years old. A beautiful and charismatic young girl standing the same way on the other side of my grandparents' fence, her features expressing the same attitude. Daring me to mess with her or disagree with one word that she'd said. I gulped this time, too.

"Okay, okay," I said after clearing my throat, putting my hands overhead in the full surrender mode. "When are we leaving?"

"I'll get us reservations for early tomorrow morning. No sense waiting until he steals another shadow, you know."

I nodded, but at the same time I began wondering exactly how we could best track him down after we arrived in what I suspected was a remote coal-mining area of Appalachia. Would the people be helpful? I pictured the dueling banjos scene from the movie *Deliverance*. And I couldn't help shuddering slightly. I knew we would have to locate him quickly to prevent any more children's spirits from being stolen.

But Bell was already thinking ahead, too. "After I get us scheduled on a plane for as early as possible tomorrow morning, I'm going to run a search and see if I can find anyplace else that our Demon has been practicing his black magic, before this recent West Virginia outbreak. I'm sure he hasn't been in quiet retirement for the last fifty years. We know he keeps young by working his moonlight rituals with children's stolen shadows. Maybe something I learn about his history since Sutter Creek will benefit us in taking him down again."

"Okay, I guess that's a good plan...," I said absently, still worried about the basic problem of first locating Mr. Black's base of operations in an unfamiliar area. It obviously wouldn't be as easy as in Sutter Creek, where he was living across the street. I scratched my head. Who in the world might be able to help us track down the Traveler?

Then I snapped my fingers exactly like Gramps used to do way back then, the light bulb coming on over my head: Of course!

I had suddenly remembered my old writing buddy, Edel Shottman, who still lived in West Virginia, in the funny hooked-shaped part closest to Virginia, Maryland, and the greater D.C. area. Edel and I had gone to Clarion together at Michigan State University back in 1979. He turned out to be an excellent fiction writer, having over the past thirty years published a pair of novels and at least forty short stories and novellas while maintaining a demanding full-time job. At the time he went to Clarion, he was a young reporter at *The Register Herald* in Beckley, West Virginia, living fairly close to the heart of the Appalachian coal country.

Now, thirty years later, he was the admired dean of West Virginia journalism, having won numerous writing awards, including a Pulitzer. And I think he was currently teaching a pair of graduate courses at the University of West Virginia at Morgantown, not too far from where he lived in Hedgesville. Edel would certainly know all the little newspapers, even the weeklies, in every cranny of the state, including those in the southwestern coal-mining region, our destination. Probably knows every publisher around there by first name. And the small-town journalists/publishers would know everyone and everything going on in their areas, and probably be privy to the local gossip about recently arrived strangers, too.

I'd get Edel to give me something like a general letter of introduction that I hoped would suffice to help gain cooperation from some of these back-woods journalists and publishers. Bell and I could rough out a plausible cover story, maybe even romance the fiction that *The Sacramento Bee* published after we thought we'd destroyed Mr. Black, sent him off to Hell. In the two follow-up *Bee* articles in 1962,

Black was portrayed as a modern Typhoid Mary, infecting the seven Sutter Creek kids with some exotic ailment before he mysteriously disappeared. Of course it would add credibility to our story that we were both personally concerned about catching the creature responsible for both Bell's sister's and our friend Miracle Bob's deaths. I bet something like that might work, validating our interest and the reason for such a long trip. And I'm sure Bell could make even the toughest investigative journalist or hard-nosed country sheriff believe in both our legitimate personal concern and the phony Typhoid Mary back-up story, too.

I chuckled out loud. We would definitely be covered nicely. And we'd find our man....

Of course the big problem was going to be: What to do with him after we found him? Capturing his shadow obviously hadn't worked so well the first time around. We'd somehow lost it in the hubbub. And it might not even be realistically possible to do this time. We had been incredibly lucky in that attic fifty years ago, in that all three of us—Bell, Gramps, and I—survived. I smiled, remembering something else important that definitely helped me back then. I'd been able to control my fear and had performed bravely in the old attic by conjuring my first ever Riastradh trance... at least I believed that's what had taken place.

I called Edel Shottman, explained the situation briefly. He said he'd pick us up tomorrow at Dulles Airport. Get him the time and the flight number tonight. He'd lend us a car, and, "Forget about a general letter of introduction." He'd take care of our meeting the "right" people with a few preliminary phone calls. He wouldn't be able to accompany us, though, because he was wrapping up a series of political-corruption articles in the next couple of days in eastern West Virginia. He might be able to catch-up with us in two or three days, if we were still down in McDowell County.

Bell came in a little later with our flight booked for 6:30 a.m. tomorrow. Two brief stops in San Francisco and Chicago, then landing at Dulles at 4:45 p.m. In addition, she had come up with some interesting information regarding some of Shadrach Black's possible travels in the last fifty years.

"Well, I could only find one probable instance of our demon surfacing, and that was fairly recently, but I dug up two other highly suggestive sightings some time ago. The first possible was about ten years after Sutter Creek, five kids getting sick in 1973 with similar symptoms, all living in a trailer park near an abandoned gypsum-mining operation in Eastern Nevada. No mention of Mr. Shadrach Black or anyone like him, though. Neaby doctors figured it was maybe a localized viral epidemic but never confirmed that. Most trailer-park locals, many of them members of ex-gypsum-miner families, blamed the small epidemic on the abandoned mining operation having polluted their drinking water...." She paused to peer at me knowingly and catch her breath, then continued.

"Mr. Black may have also surfaced around one of the last Comstock Lode silver-mining operations in Western Nevada, in 1978. Details are sketchy, but a Virginia City weekly newspaper there suggested that a forty-year–old vagabond may have been carrying some kind of rare super bug and infected a string of children in the area...."

She again paused, lifted her eyebrows into sharp inverted Vs, nodded, and smiled questioningly. Uh-huh, a vagabond and a super bug, you say?

"But the best possibility surfaced about six years ago, near the San Onofre nuclear reactor in Southern California. Seven kids were hospitalized over a nine-month period with almost identical symptoms as at Sutter Creek. Three eventually died from liver and kidney failure, before a suspicious man moved on. Sound familiar? Some figured this guy may've been carrying some exotic disease, because a semi-coherent victim claimed the man made some direct physical contact with him, just before the boy got sick: "He captured my spirit." And there was a pretty good local description that fit our Mr. Shadrach Black to a T. But there was also, again, a distracting, noisy explanation circulating in the community about childhood leukemia caused by the temporarily shutdown nuclear reactor. Quite an uproar, in fact. The highly vocal anti-nuke crowd joined some of the parental protesters and their friends. Lots of on-line coverage by the local *Valley News*. But I could find only the briefest follow-up in national newspapers or the news services, and that was relegated to a few back pages." She stopped and shrugged apologetically.

"This is all I turned up tonight, but our Demon's undoubtedly been busy, operating continuously since we exposed him fifty years ago. And he's successfully kept under the radar ever since, covering his M.O."

"Yes, and I bet he does that by specifically picking places in rural areas that have been polluted by some unpopular corporation, in order to deflect initial attention away from his shadow stealing. Seems that way to me, anyhow."

Bell nodded. "I think you're probably right and…." She shrugged dismissively. " Of course these small towns wouldn't have the fastest-reacting law enforcement or health authorities either. Probably severely undermanned. Maybe relying mostly on neighboring, more populated and better-equipped towns or counties for technical assistance."

"That sounds about right to me."

We both thought the situation over for a few moments.

Then, Bell interrupted my thoughts by announcing: "Oh, I'll have some other research I've been digging up specifically on demons, hopefully available to discuss on the plane tomorrow. I started with the word, *Genie*. Led to some intriguing stuff regarding the Middle-Eastern Romany and their legendary Djinns—*Genie* is derived from the Arabic word. Especially one Djinn in particular. I'm attempting to run down more specific information on him. This might turn out to be real good." She smiled.

I said: "All sounds great, kiddo. Good work. But I better get back to Edel before it gets too late there in West Virginia."

I called my friend back with our flight information and ETA. He already had some things nearly lined up for us. I listened for a couple of minutes.

After I hung up, I filled Bell in: "Edel is going to meet us at Dulles Airport. We'll go home with him, make a follow-up call and, if necessary an appointment that same night—depending on the outcome of one more important call he wants to make. He says he hopes to introduce us to the legendary Doris Dunnigan, in Bradshaw, McDowell County.

"Eighty-four-year-old Miss Dee Dee, as everyone calls her down there, owns and publishes the weekly, and has been doing so for over forty years. Her sarcastically entertaining syndicated column on national political affairs appears regularly in larger papers all over West Virginia and the greater Washington D.C. area, maybe some other parts of the country, too. But the *Record,* her baby, was the first to report the mysterious ailment affecting the four kids in a hospital nearby. Miss Dee Dee is the Molly Ivens of West Virginia, loved and respected throughout the state and the D.C. area, just like Molly was down in Texas and Washington before she died.

"Miss Dee Dee first focused national attention on the coal miners' plight over three decades ago, and during the process won several journalistic awards for her investigative series, including one on the dreaded Black Lung Disease. She helped win the first monetary court awards against the mining companies for miner families. But in the last couple of years she's been publishing editorials commending the mining corporations for their recent positive environmental efforts to clean up dangerous tailing messes. Steps in the right direction. She's a first-class, fair journalist by any standard.

"Anyhow, I told Edel a skimpy cover story about what we were doing. Focused on your sister and Miracle Bob being infected by this guy and then dying. We're going down there to try to track down the carrier of this disease, a modern day Typhoid Mary. Edel said we could count on cooperation from Miss Dee Dee, who is still plenty sharp even though she is confined to a wheel-chair, and living with an amputated foot and failing vision from her battle with diabetes. Even with her own physical problems, she is deeply concerned with this potential children's epidemic in her community. Edel says we may find her to be, I think he said, a cranky rustic....

"With her help, I have the feeling we'll find our Demon quickly, if he's still around there somewhere."

"I bet he is," Bell said. "However his spirit stealing goes, it seems to work best after he's accumulated at least seven shadows, like in Sutter Creek and again at San Onofre, and, who knows, probably other places, too."

I nodded and sucked in a deep breath, realizing I was feeling pretty unsettled by the onslaught of all this sudden stress. With a moment of downtime to think, I was having a tough time focusing and gearing up mentally to put on a full court press on the entity we called, Shadrach Black. Pretty shaky, in fact.

"I'm really on edge tonight, pretty unnerved about all this, kiddo," I finally admitted. "I thought this nightmare was over, you know, buried in our past. But here we go again, battling what is probably a manifestation of a true Demon. Jesus, I may be just getting a bit too out of shape for this sort of stuff, you know. I'm close to being a sedentary senior citizen now, spending my days sitting on my ass writing...."

She peered at me and slowly shook her head. Then she nodded with a sly seductiveness blended with that old Bell look of super-confidence, and said: "Come on over here, Big Boy, and put your face right here." She marked a spot near her face, using the cherished words from so long ago.

I chuckled, flashing back to that first time in Sutter Creek at my grandparent's fence....

And, of course, again I responded to Bell's command.

The long kiss was quite a bit different this time, though. Wet and arousing. As we broke apart, she said: "Senior citizen...you think?"

Of course I immediately forgot about that sweet incident in the past and wasn't laughing at all as this very sexy woman led me off to bed. At sixty-two, she possessed a lot more than just a cocky attitude. She still had an extremely attractive body and some sensually provocative moves. Oh, yeah!

Part II
West Virginia

Chapter 11

River Community Hit Hard

Upper Dry Fork, a proud community of 76 people and near as many coon dogs in northern McDowell County has been hit hard recently with more than its fair share of tragedy. Flooding almost every year since the turn of the 21st century. And highly respected Community spokesman, Nate Whitethorn, finally losing his battle and succumbing to Black Lung Disease over eight months ago. And since then, a string of four youngsters have fallen ill to a mysterious ailment. So serious that all are now in ICU at Welch Community Hospital, 27 miles from their remote riverside homes. To date the exact nature of their medical disorder has not been identified, despite consultation and some sophisticated testing by notable specialists from the medical school at the University of West Virginia in Morgantown. Several theories are being explored, ranging from trying to identify a rare super bug not indigenous to the county, to again blaming the recently departed coal mining companies. Of course, these corporate villains have been held responsible in recent years for everything from our bad weather to our poor church attendance. So, hey, why not hold them accountable for the plight of our four severely ill youngsters?

—*McDowell County Record,* October 5, 2012

October 11, 2012—In-flight Sacramento to Dulles, Virginia

After we got settled on our cross-country flight, Bell produced a manila folder from her carry-on and dug out a legal-sized yellow sheet crammed full of notes she'd scribbled down late last night after I'd gone to sleep.

"This is some intriguing stuff, Sean, and I suspect it will be pretty important when we run down Mr. Shadrach Black," she said, pointing at her notes. "This goes back to ancient times, involving the myths of a small Romany culture in the Mideast. Their legendary demons were called Djinns in Arabic. Satan himself is the most infamous Djinn from this early period. But we are interested in another, much less prominent demon, one I found referenced in a rare tome, *Ancient Babylonian Lore*. His name was Bezeki.

"A demon—now get this, pal—who only cast a shadow in the moonlight, never during the day. He preferred the dark and cold, and was usually only seen at night, avoiding sunlight and heat. It's claimed he nourished his dark inner essence by draining the shadow-spirits of young children. But I found no specific details on exactly how he accomplished that. You know, nothing about him stealing shadows, or moonlight rituals, or strange incantations, or what have you...."

Her voice trailed off as she peered at me, arching her eyebrows, and then going on in her Bell voice: "Sean, I'm convinced that this legendary Djinn is now in West Virginia and that he is none other than our own Shadrach Black."

I nodded, thought a moment, and asked a question: "Anything in your notes about how to get this Genie back into the bottle?"

She smiled thinly, while still looking concerned, and said, "No, nothing on that. But just like your Gramps suspected about dealing with Shadrach Black in Sutter Creek, conventional weapons and methods don't seem to have ever worked against any Mideastern Djinn down through the ages." Her concerned expression eased as she added: "But the good news is every Djinn seems to have an Achilles heel that can be exploited, if one is clever enough to discover the nature of the fatal weakness."

I was getting excited now, because I realized that Bell's research was doubtlessly right-on. Our demon was this ancient Babylonian Djinn, Bezeki. And while reflecting on the notes that Bell had just shared, I also realized that Gramps had been correct on another assumption about

Shadrach Black. He'd felt from early on that the Traveler hated the sun and the heat. That he avoided it as much as possible, always bundling up like a desert Bedouin whenever out during daytime. Could this be the Djinn's Achilles' heel—sunlight and heat?

During the remainder of the first major leg of our flight, the last two plus hours from San Francisco to Chicago, we discussed how we might be able to use this new information. How we could best neutralize the Djinn? We went around and around, coming to only one definite conclusion: Conventional weapons like guns were most likely useless. But we were unable to come up with any constructive plan. Bell kept dwelling on how we'd initially captured the demon's night shadow. By using the spotlight. But she felt we'd actually screwed up complete success by letting the captured shadow slip out of our hands.

Maybe we could catch the demon's shadow again, she suggested, and this time somehow permanently destroy it. I argued that I couldn't see how we'd be able to easily fool the demon a second time, and maneuver him into a similar position, enabling us to capture his night shadow. He'd obviously be more wary; he'd avoid getting trapped in an enclosed dark space, where we could use a strong beam and capture his night shadow. And I couldn't help coming back to what seemed to me to offer the most promising avenue to success: exposing Bezeki directly to the sun and heat of day.

But of course, this general possibility would require a much more detailed plan and then proper execution. We both readily admitted that there might be something else here we were missing, something much easier to execute and more likely to succeed. But neither of us could come up with even one other promising alternative. I felt we weren't doing our best creative thinking while in the air. So, we finally decided to shut the discussion down. We'd give it more thought after we were on the ground.

We both actually rested the second major leg of the flight from Chicago on to Dulles, and I even drifted off.

October 11, 2012—

Edel Shottman picked us up at Dulles International Airport at 5:15 that evening, our continuing flight from Chicago into the D.C. area having arrived a bit late.

He looked about the same as the last time I'd seen him, two years ago at a horror writer's convention in Austin, Texas. Perhaps a few more flecks of gray in his full black beard and additional gray streaks above his ears, and maybe a pound or two heavier. He was a large, husky man, the poster image of a West Virginia Mountaineer. But despite his six-four frame and rugged lumberjack appearance, Edel was a witty, kind-hearted, generous individual—actually more of a teddy than a grizzly bear.

We took off in his 1998 Bonneville sedan, a vintage vehicle that matched his scruffy but classic looks. Initially, we made slow progress through heavy traffic. He explained that, being caught like this in the evening commute, it might take as much as two hours to reach his home near Hedgesville, West Virginia. Neither Bell nor I had ever been out here, so Edel gave us a journalist's rundown on information of general interest, and a few relevant facts that might be useful later on.

"Appalachia appears on the map of the United States running northeast to southwest. It includes parts of Kentucky, Tennessee, Virginia, Maryland, North Carolina, and almost all of West Virginia. Despite living in West Virginia, I don't consider myself an inhabitant of Appalachia; more like a resident of an extended Maryland bedroom community. Lots of folk commuting daily into the D.C. area from out here...."

He indicated the passing scenery out the window. Even in the rapidly falling autumn dusk, we could see the countryside was turning rural, hilly, and heavily wooded.

Edel continued: "Of course you folks from the West, with your massive Rockies and Sierra Nevadas, probably don't consider Appalachia to be real mountains. But if they are only hills, they are definitely steep, isolating hills, harboring some really rugged country. With a grand variety of native trees. You already know West Virginia is renowned as part of the country's best coal region. But where you are headed, in the very southwestern corner of the State, are some of the most extensive deposits of bituminous coal perhaps in the entire USA. Both a bounty in the past and a bane for the folks still living there. The large coal companies have done damage to some of the most magnificent parts of the State by Mountain Top Strip Mining. MTSM has left terrible environmental scars, even worse than the littered swaths of clear-cut logging in your Pacific Northwest forests. You can replant clear-cut areas and the secondary timber growth will eventually recover. But there is no practical and economic way to rebuild partially leveled mountains.

"You are headed for an area that generally prospered in past decades, despite the individual coal miners' deplorable working conditions, low pay, and poor benefits. They had steady work. Now that the coal mining corporations are mostly gone, McDowell County is the most impoverished spot in West Virginia, perhaps one of the poorest in all of America. In the last forty years the county population has shrunk from well over one hundred thousand to under twenty-four thousand. Bradshaw, the county seat has less than five hundred people living there now. The average yearly family income in the county is way below the country's poverty level, only about $9,500 at best…."

Edel paused again and shook his head, with a concerned frown deeply creasing his wrinkled forehead. "These people have experienced more than their share of tragedy over recent decades. Extensive flooding of their homes. Trapped miners. Killed miners. Disabled miners. Black Lung Disease. Unemployment ranging from the low-to-mid-30s. Poor schools. Poor diets. You name it.

"But always proud, self-reliant folks. What they don't need now is some kind of exotic epidemic taking down their children. Of course Miss Dee Dee understands all this. She's lived it. She'll help all she can to find this guy you're looking for. And she'll get Junior McDowell to cooperate, too, or at least stay out of your way. He's the county sheriff down there, from a historic line. You'll find him a bag of peanuts short of a Southwest Airlines plane ride and not really too ambitious either, but jovial and well-intentioned, considering he's pretty much resigned to living off his family name."

October 12, 2012—

We spent the night at Edel's place, getting an early start the next morning, fortified with a hearty breakfast and a good map for our six-plus-hour drive clear across the state, to Bradshaw, the county seat of impoverished McDowell County.

As Edel had indicated, the countryside was indeed glorious, steeply rugged and heavily forested mountains. Covered with familiar small stands of oak, laurel, and pine, but mostly a variety of other trees not commonly found in far west mountains, like ash, spruce, sycamore, and sugar maple. And as we drove into the heart of coal-mining Appalachia we saw some examples of the terrible scarring of MTSM, which probably also contributed to heavy erosion and the severe flooding of the small communities built along the banks of creeks and rivers. Some of this Edel had briefly warned us about last night. But the actual first-hand exposure to the stark devastation of this kind of coal mining was shocking. As we neared our destination, the unscarred, steep, heavily wooded mountains were splattered with a brilliant palette of fall colors. The wide swathes of golden sugar maple leaves were complemented with striking dabs of scarlet, burnt orange, mahogany, and rust. Colorful, gorgeous, breathtaking country.

Hard to believe that somewhere in these mountains an ancient children's-spirit-stealing Djinn was lurking.

Around two o'clock we drove down the Main Street of Bradshaw, a line of buildings on both sides of the road. The narrow town rested in a steep cleft between two thickly forested mountains. The nearby junction of Bradshaw Creek and the Dry Fork River hampered growth, and, in addition, created potential annual flooding problems for the lower parts of the town.

We continued on the Bradshaw-Grundy Road to the nearby community of Grundy and found our motel room in a fairly modern Comfort Inn, which Edel had reserved for us. Where we freshened up before returning to Bradshaw for our scheduled 4:00 meeting with Miss Dee Dee at the address for the *County Record*.

Chapter 12

October 12, 2012—

The office of the *County Record* turned out to be a large, first-floor study located in Miss Dee Dee's wood-framed, two-story Colonial. The beautifully walnut-paneled room was crowded with overflowing bookshelves, with stacks of papers, journals, and state-report binders littering every chair, and more than three quarters of the floor space. She did all of her writing on a desk computer, the weekly newspaper actually printed and distributed from larger Beckley in nearby Raleigh County.

Miss Dee Dee rested in her wheelchair, resembling a typical grandmotherly, heavyset woman…nondescript until she opened her mouth to ask questions. Her soft-spoken voice was steady, precise, and probing. But we would soon discover it was occasionally spiked with a jarring outburst of profanity that would've shocked a Marine Drill Sergeant.

"Okay, so much for getting acquainted. Edel explained during his phone call last night why you two are nosing around my county. Why don't you both clear a chair, sit back, relax, and elaborate a bit more for me. Why exactly did you take such a long trip across the country to land here?"

Bell nodded, took a deep breath, exhaled, and proceeded into her long-winded song and dance about tracking a male Typhoid Mary, who was responsible for infecting and killing both her sister and our best friend with an unidentified disease back in Sutter Creek, California in 1962.

"And you actually recognized him here in Bradshaw on the TV late last night? This guy you've just described to me? With his bushy black eyebrows and his deep-set black eyes and all the rest of that? You think he's here in our county?"

We both nodded.

From her manila folder, Bell produced a printout of last night's Bradshaw Courthouse audience scene, downloaded from the TV. Shadrach Black was in the middle of the group, and Bell had carefully circled him in red.

The famed journalist squinted her eyes, bent over, and studied the reproduced pic for only a brief moment with her thick glasses pushed high up on her forehead. After finishing, she handed the pic back to Bell.

"Okay, let me see if I've got all this straight...," Miss Dee Dee finally said, pausing and peering intently at me for a moment with her glasses still resting atop her head, then letting her unwavering gaze shift to Bell. "You recognized him as the same man from back when you were kids in Sutter Creek...about fifty years ago, is that correct?"

Bell began to answer: "Yes—"

"Bullshit!"

Miss Dee Dee was shaking her head vigorously and frowning angrily. Looking nothing like a soft-spoken, kindly, chubby grandmother type resting in a wheelchair. "I think your whole story is a contrived load of bull-pucky, and it smells to high heaven."

We both sat up stiffly, not really having a response to her scatological outburst.

"If some guy infected those kids in Sutter Creek back in 1962, he'd be older than me, at least ninety by now, maybe a bit older. You two expect me to believe he still looks to be in his late thirties like you just described him, and he obviously appears in this reproduction? I may look like a doddering old dumbbell...but I got news for you two smooth-talking city slickers. My bullshit detector is still every bit as reliable as Ernest Hemingway's. Okay? Now, if you really want my full cooperation, you need to knock-off the bullcrap and level with me; and I mean the whole frigging story, as you understand it. You hear me?" She sagged back in her wheelchair, but her expression was still confrontational.

We sat dumbfounded for a few seconds.

Of course the old lady was right. Bad eyes or not, she had deconstructed our cover story in less than five seconds after looking at the pic. Shadrach Black would have aged fifty-some years. He wouldn't look anything like our description, or like the guy circled in the print from TV. We sure wouldn't have been able to recognize him as an old man last night, especially in a clustered, dark, brief grainy shot like that. We'd screwed-up our cover story, underestimated folks here in general, and disrespected this renowned, award-winning journalist. The old lady had easily spotted the preposterous weak link and the rest quickly fell apart. She was super sharp, just like Edel had warned. And a cranky rustic. We should have listened closer.

I glanced at Bell, who sucked in a deep breath, shrugged, and nodded at me. "Might as well tell her the whole frigging story, Sean, the detailed version."

After a moment, I said: "Okay, Miss Dee Dee, this is the true story, as inexplicable as it may sound...."

For the next forty-five minutes or so, I carefully described the the shadow-capturing incidents at Sutter Creek when we were kids. How we finally trapped what we thought was an Irish Traveler in the attic and freed the seven shadows. But too late to save Miracle Bob and Lettie. I even updated the story by including Bell's discovery of three subsequent possible sightings of the man we knew as Shadrach Black. And everything we knew about a Babylonian Djinn named Bezeki. I finally finished, and shrugged in supplication, my palms held up to the old journalist.

She didn't go off again as I thought she might; instead she sat quietly for a few long moments. Then Miss Dee Dee smiled, not unkindly. She scratched the back of her head vigorously, before she spoke in her normal voice.

"Well, here in these back woods, I've listened to dozens of country folk's vividly told stories that involved all manner of bizarre supernatural strangeness. Hell's Bells, even heard described a few alien abductions over the years. But, I have to admit that yours is definitely the weirdest story I've ever heard, tops them all without question."

At that point she chuckled loudly and winked at me. "Make the basis of a Goddamned exciting novel for you, Sean O'Donnell; and who knows, maybe another award winner." Which suggested she'd done a little prior background checking on my literary bona fides, including the two awards.

Then, a serious expression slowly crept onto her face. "Don't really matter what I think about the veracity of your story, as long as I'm convinced you believe it. And, more important, you believe you can catch this...ah, Djinn, and save our kids." At that point her hard-edged expression eased into a thin smile. "And I guess by now I'm a pretty damned good judge of character, so, yes, I believe you are both sincere in wanting to catch this guy, whoever he might actually prove to be. I believe you want to save our kids. So I'll do everything in my power to help you do that. What's up first?"

After a moment, Bell cleared her voice and said: "Well, we are going to need someone to introduce us around Upper Dry Fork. A person the community will trust, because we want to show that TV pic around to them and their children. We're betting someone has spotted this character, because he's obviously been stealing shadows up there, for at least the last six months. Anyone like that readily come to mind, Miss Dee Dee?"

The old lady reached over and picked up her phone.

"Buddy?" she said. "I have an assignment for you.... Yes, come to the office as soon as you finish."

She hung up and explained: "Buddy McPhee is a very good investigative reporter for the *Record*. And my legs, so to speak. He hails from Upper Dry Fork. In fact, one of the four stricken youngsters in the hospital is his nephew. You can meet him here shortly, after he finishes his dinner. And then, if it works out for everyone concerned, the three of you might want to go up to Upper Dry Fork tomorrow morning and check around. Sound like a reasonable plan?"

"Great," I said, realizing that Buddy McPhee was just what we needed, a local middleman with a vested interest in catching our demon.

Buddy McPhee was older than his nickname might have implied. Maybe early forties. He wore a gold-and-blue collegiate West Virginia sweatshirt—maybe a lifelong football fan of the Mountaineers.

After we greeted him, Miss Dee Dee brought him up to speed, repeating the critical points of our story about tracking down a supernatural creature responsible for stealing kids' shadows, which made them sick. He didn't roll an eye or chuckle dismissively as he listened. Apparently, the famous old journalist's involvement in this operation was all the validation our story required from Buddy McPhee.

When the old lady finished her explanation, and spelled out what she wanted from him, he simply said, "Okay, I'm onboard one hundred percent, Miss Dee Dee."

"Good man," the old journalist said, with a broad smile.

October 13, 2012—

The next morning, Bell, Buddy, and I drove the ten miles from Bradshaw to Upper Dry Fork. Along a narrow, winding old county road. The mountain settlement was little more than a dozen or so wood-framed buildings strung in a line along a short bluff, which eventually sloped down to a rushing creek. The town ended with several wide-body trailers clustered at its far northern end. In the center of the line of residences was a tiny grocery store with a small flagpole out front and a neatly lettered black-and-white sign in the window: "USPS & Megan's Mart."

We parked in front of Megan's.

We had a leisurely cup of coffee at the grocery counter, chatting with the attractive owner of the market, Megan Whitethorn, showing our reproduced pic to her. During the remainder of the morning, we would show that pic to four more people who wandered in to pick up groceries and collect their mail at an official-looking, red-white-and-blue barred window at the end of the counter. No one at the store, including Megan, recognized our man; and no one remembered seeing a stranger about town recently. Apparently, our Shadrach Black was keeping his head down.

Then we got lucky.

About 11:30, Buddy took us to his youngest sister's place, one of the wide-body, aluminum-sided trailers sitting on large cinder blocks. He introduced us to Allyson and her eight-year-old daughter, Irma, who was being kept home from school in Bradshaw because of a sudden outbreak of sore throats and drippy noses—parents here were apparently super-protective of their kids since the mysterious disease broke out. After exchanging family pleasantries, Buddy showed them the TV pic and asked if they recognized the man circled.

Allyson shook her head. "Nope. 'Fraid not, Buddy. Sorry."

But Buddy's niece, a shy, rosy-cheeked little girl, tucked in tightly at her mom's hip, nodded.

"You've seen this man, Irma?" Buddy asked, a trace of excitement in his voice.

The youngster whispered: "Yes, I have, Uncle Buddy. Me and Josh both saw him. When we were fishing upstream." She pointed north into the forest. Josh was her eleven-year-old brother, one of the four youngsters in the ICU at Welch Community Hospital.

"Was this real soon before Josh got sick?" Buddy asked.

The little girl thought a moment and nodded.

She said: "Josh got sick the very next day, right after he went fishing again by himself. Papa had to rush him to the hospital."

Bell interrupted and asked Buddy: "Anyone live up there where the kids fish?"

Buddy slowly shook his head. But, after a moment's thought, he added: "Wait—actually, there is a dilapidated cabin up there. The old Turner place."

Silence for a long moment.

"Okay," Buddy said to his relatives after turning from Bell and me, "your information is very helpful. Thank you kindly."

"Yes, indeed," I said, nodding at the woman and her daughter.

"Thank you very much, Irma and Allyson," Bell added, easing toward the trailer door.

Buddy kissed his sister and niece before following us, saying: "I'll get back to you soon."

Outside the trailer, I asked: "You know where this Turner place is located, right, Buddy?"

"Sure do," he said. "Isn't very far at all, up near the rapids. Easy walking distance from here along the county road."

We followed the road for about a half of a mile, going deeper into the woods and passing no buildings or trailers, until we finally reached the Turner property. After spotting the small building, we stood on the side of a broad clearing, catching our breath and cautiously searching about.

The building was a small, ramshackle cabin, set back about a hundred yards from the rushing creek. It rested on the far side of the clearing in the dark, cool, quiet of the lengthening shadows, not even a bird or squirrel disturbing the gloomy peace.

A few minutes passed.

We stealthily appproached the front of the one-room shack, all our senses on full alert.

The cabin door hung slightly ajar.

I pushed the door wider, and we peered into the gloomy interior—

Screech.

A blur of gray shot past my leg, startling everyone.

It was only a frightened cat!

I took a deep breath, let it out slowly, and sighed, my blood thumping in my ears.

It didn't feel like anyone was here…or had been for quite a few years. Maybe the cat, or other small animals like squirrels or rats, had used it for shelter, because there were debris strewn across the floor, and some of the stuffing from a dirty quilt was piled in the corner like a nest. The wooden bunk-bed frame in another corner was damaged, resting aslant, a leg completely snapped off. The single cupboard was bare of food or dishes. Not much else to see.

"I'm guessing your man has not been living here recently," Buddy said, his dry humor reflecting the obvious.

Neither Bell nor I bothered to explain that our Mr. Shadrach Black didn't leave much of a mark wher he stayed. He could be using this cabin—or the nearby area—as his center of operations. Especially if kids were coming up this way to fish. It was isolated. He could steal their shadows with impunity.

We searched outside the shack, finding nothing but an old, rusty axe buried in a stump chopping-block on the path to the outhouse, which was more broken-down than the shack.

It got dark and cold early in the forest. So we decided to return to the *Record* office, regroup, and plan out our next move.

Chapter 13

October 13, 2012—

"No, unfortunately we didn't find any evidence that Shadrach Black was living at the Turner Cabin," I explained to Miss Dee Dee. Buddy had already told her that no adult we'd talked to in Upper Dry Fork had seen a stranger recently, but that his niece, Irma, thought she'd seen our man, when she was fishing with her brother—had, in fact, seen him the day before Josh came down sick and had to be hospitalized.

The old journalist smiled sardonically. "Well, he's definitely been spotted here in Bradshaw, at least twice, about six or seven months ago. Got Junior to show that pic of yours around, after I bribed him with a quart of coffee and three donuts."

"Where did they see him?" Bell asked.

We were sitting in the *Record* office, drinking hot coffee laced with a drop or two of Miss Dee Dee's strictly medicinal Bushmills. The outside temperature had dropped after sunset, and the Irish-whiskey-fortified drink knocked the edge off the chill.

"At Jacob's Hardware," Miss Dee Dee said. "First time, he was picking up some tools—handsaw, hammer, screwdriver, nails, screws, two-by-fours, and several sheets of plywood. A couple of weeks later, he returned and picked up a small sheet of plywood, some spackling, a long extension cord, a couple of rolls of duct tape, and a key-hole saw—"

"Yes!" I snapped my fingers, realizing at that moment how we could pinpoint the location of his hideout. Where he was storing those four kids' frozen shadows.

Excited, I followed up with a question: "Miss Dee Dee, do they stock generators in that little hardware store?"

She looked at Buddy, her eyebrows raised.

"I don't think so, anymore," he replied. "Nothing as slow-moving or expensive as that, at least since the mines closed down. But I bet you could special order one at Jacob's, and get it delivered from Beckley anywhere in the County, maybe even the next day."

"Think you could check out Jacob's again and see if our man special ordered a generator on either of those visits?" I asked. "And if he did, where was it delivered?"

"I'll head right over. They should be open for a bit more," Buddy said, taking a copy of the pic to show again at the hardware store.

"All right, pal, that's the kind of sharp thinking we need!" Bell said, knowing exactly what I had in mind.

After getting back from the hardware store, Buddy announced with a big grin: "You were right, Sean. Mr. Jacobs himself dug through the special order receipts. On his second visit, your guy, under the name Hubert Jones, ordered a gas-fueled generator. He had it dropped off at the doorstep of the Turner Cabin, exactly five and a half months ago, on June 2nd. On that same visit, he copied some information from the bulletin board about a used portable refrigeration unit for sale here in Bradshaw."

I explained to Buddy and Miss Dee Dee why I thought Hubert Jones needed a generator and a refrigeration unit. Buddy looked taken aback, rubbing his face and murmuring: "Kids' frozen shadows?"

But the old journalist cut right to the chase.

"But today you found no generator at the Turner cabin, I assume," Miss Dee Dee said.

I shook my head. "No, but he must have set up the generator close by. It'd be too bulky and heavy for one person to move far, even with a wheelbarrow. Same with the cooling unit. And he couldn't have used any help, not wanting to reveal the location of his hideout. If possible he'd set that equipment up where he didn't think the generator's humming would attract anyone's attention."

It was silent for a few moments, everyone turning over in their heads what I'd just suggested.

"You know," Miss Dee Dee finally said, staring absently at a stack of dusty reports in the corner. "I recall an old mine shaft dug up there...oh, back when most men around here were working long shifts at the companies' mines. But a few individuals, including Rory Turner and his two brothers, owned the mineral rights and sub-rights to their properties. They conducted a small, independent mining operation for themselves. Did pretty well for quite a while, as I recall, until one of the big companies finally bought them out. Anyhow, I'll bet that old shaft is still up there. Be a good spot, I think, for this Hubert Jones to hide out, set up shop, and operate from."

She described to Buddy where we might find the shaft. I figured that a producing mine being up there explained the old county road, extended—at some expense—to the isolated Turner Cabin, so coal tonnage could be hauled to the railroad in Bradshaw.

October 14, 2012—

The next morning, Bell and I met with Buddy to talk about going to the old mine shaft. We needed to develop a plan for catching Hubert Jones, if we did find him and the four shadows. Miss Dee Dee thought we might want to take Junior McDowell with us—some armed muscle. We were kicking that idea around when we heard a loud, whooping sound outside.

At first I thought it was a cop-car siren in front of the *Record*.

But the shrill sound lingered and echoed loudly through the entire town.

Before I could ask about it, though, Buddy held up his hand, and took a call on his cell phone.

"C'mon," he said, "volunteer-fire-department stuff. Little grass fire south of town. Won't take much time, and you guys can watch how us backwoods amateurs put out a fire."

We followed him a block uptown to a metal shed housing an old but nicely polished red pumper. Two men and a woman arrived about the same time as Buddy but ignored the fire engine. They picked up shovels and heavy backpacks and piled into the bed of one of the men's pickup truck.

Bell, I, and a stream of other gawkers followed on foot to a grass fire burning in a field about twenty-five yards south of town.

By then, the four volunteer firefighters had struggled into their backpacks, which resembled pest-control equipment—a container on the back, with a hose extending around to a long, hand-held spray nozzle. Except these firefighters hand-pumped high-pressure streams of water as far as twenty-five yards, the heavy backpacks containing a ten-gallon supply of water. They had the fire under control in under five minutes. They finished by carefully the smoking ashes with shovelfuls of dirt.

After they were sure the fire was completely out, the four began joking, laughing, and congratulating themselves, like a winning bowling team, as they climbed back into the bed of the Ford F-150 for the brief ride to the fire station.

Watching them use the accurate portable water extinguishers stirred the germ of an idea. I hadn't been able to figure out a good way to lure the demon into the sunlight and heat; but possibly, just maybe, I could bring the sun to him.

"Bell, I want to go to the fire station for a few minutes," I said, as we neared the *County Record*. "I want to check out an idea for getting rid of our Djinn. See if the critical part is even feasible. You want to come along?"

"If we're going up there this afternoon, I better get some sandwiches and things. Might be there quite a while, you know. I'll meet you at Miss Dee Dee's in a few minutes. Then you can tell us your plan. Okay?" She knew I was pretty stoked.

I left her crossing the street and heading over to Bradshaw's main grocery store, Food-Mart.

I nearly bounced out of the fire station, because by the experts had judged an important component of my scheme to be viable. I described my complete plan for taking down Bezeki as I walked back with Buddy from the fire station. He liked it, even though he had a piece of equipment we could use. He said it hadn't been used for years, and the family jokingly called it "Grandpa's old iron." I couldn't wait to lay out the plan to Bell.

A block away from the *County Record*, I saw Bell emerge from the grocery store, carrying a small, full brown bag, and take a few steps easterly. I waved to catch her attention.

She stopped to cross the street, waiting for a break in traffic, and as she looked to her left she spotted me.

She returned my wave—

That's when I saw a frightening face in the alley at the western end of the store, behind Bell.

Shadrach Black!

The recognition was like a punch to the stomach and made me gasp for air.

He was peering at a spot behind Bell…at her shadow, extending toward the alley.

Jesus! I could sense what Black was thinking. My heart thumped, my pulse raced, my throat tightened up, and as I blinked…I heard my grandfather's brogue: *You have to help Bell! Right now, Sean boy!*

Everything began to unfold in surrealistic, NFL TV slow motion.

In hat and duster, Black crept ominously toward Bell's shadow.

"Run! Bell, run!" I shouted, each word requiring a maximum effort to get out, as I pointed behind her.

Taking an eternity, she finally turned and spotted Shadrach Black…and understood.

As she flung her grocery bag into the air, it seemed to stall for a moment, defying gravity…then she was twisting toward me, extending her hand, as if trying to reach across the street for my help. She prepared to run, dropping into a partial sprinter's crouch….

Too late.

Shadrach Black leapt into the air, floating down like a paratrooper, and landing solidly on the head of Bell's shadow with both of his feet—those glossy black wingtips.

I heard Bell gasp in pain.

She froze in place, as if she'd suddenly been paralyzed.

I raced toward her, feeling as if I were shackled to an invisible ball and chain. Slowly, too slowly, I made it half way across the street.

Black bent…and—agonized—I watched his long fingers clutch and then rip Bell's shadow upward.

The sound grated painfully on my ears, raising the hair on my neck.

I struggling toward them, dragging my weighted foot and shouting a broken string of commands to the demon: "Stop…right…there…you!"

I was less than twenty-five feet away when Shadrach Black stared directly at me with his bushy eyebrows and ancient black eyes…and for the longest moment he just grinned, exactly as he had that night so long ago in Sutter Creek standing in the middle of the seven shadows, when he glanced up at the full moon—

Suddenly, his expression hardened as he dismissed my commands by spitting out, "Gadjos!"

The Romany word seemed to speed things back to normal time.

I was sprinting now, closing the distance between us…but I was too late.

With Bell's shadow flung casually over his shoulder, the Djinn disappeared into the dark alleyway.

I couldn't follow, because Bell was lying limply at the edge of the street.

I reached her and bent over, touching her face gently, my throat tight, my eyes blurring. "Bell, Bell, are you all right?" I murmured in a choked voice.

She responded with a long, deep sigh, and then closed her eyes. She was unconscious.

Buddy was at my side by then. "Sean, we need to get her over to the ER in Welch. Quickly."

I nodded, scooped my wife up in my arms, and hurried to the *County Record,* where Buddy's Dodge Ram pickup was parked.

We wrapped Bell into a warm blanket and rested her head in my lap in the pickup bed.

Buddy sped off to Welch Community Hospital, over twenty miles away.

It seemed an eternity before the ER doctor came out to talk to me.

"Mr. O'Donnell?" His name tag read, "Dr. Browning."

"Yes."

"Your wife is as stable as possible."

"She's doing well, going to be okay?"

"Perhaps not," Dr. Browning said, shrugging slightly. "The symptoms are similar to those of four children in the ICU. But the prognosis may be quite different. Mrs. O'Donnell's symptoms seem much more acute, and her vital signs are challengingly low. Probably because of her age—"

"Challengingly low?"

"We are doing everything possible with what to help the four youngsters a bit. Blood transfusions, antibiotics, painkillers, several other medications, and …."

His voice trailed off.

I shook my head and pressed him. "'Challengingly low' means exactly what, Dr. Browning? Give it to me straight, please."

He sucked in a deep breath, visibly distressed. "Well, we hope she responds to the blood transfusions and medications. But if she doesn't, and her vital signs continue to erode…." He paused again, obviously dreading stating the obvious conclusion. He reached out, gently gripped my shoulder, squeezed, and added: "In the next twenty-four, maybe thirty-six hours at most, those signs must stabilize or we will lose her—"

"You mean Bell could die in the next day or so?"

The doctor didn't respond for a few moments. Then he said: "I'm sorry, Mr. O'Donnell."

I nodded, tried to swallow.

Jesus, I swore silently, sighing deeply.

For a few moments I was too numbed to think…then I heard Gramps clearly again: *Quit feeling sorry for yourself, boyo, time to get busy.*

He was right, of course.

It was critical that we find Shadrach Black's hideout…and free Bell's shadow. Within the next twenty-four hours. The clock was ticking.

At that low moment, an old friend walked into the ER waiting room.

Chapter 14

October 14, 2012—

Edel Shottman!

His big bear hug was comforting.

"What's going on?" he asked.

I brought him briefly up to date on Bell's dire condition but suggested we go to Miss Dee Dee's, where I could fully explain what happened. And what was required to make her well.

At the *Record* office, I began my explanation to Edel: "You will be skeptical of what I'm about to say, because it's a supernatural explanation of what's happened to Bell. But bear with me, please. The solution I'm proposing to save her is one I believe in one hundred percent." I stopped a moment and added: "And I need your support and help, my friend."

He nodded and beckoned me continue.

To his credit, Edel didn't flinch during what must have sounded like an incredible story. Nor did he bat an eye as I described the gruesome measures I had in mind for when we found Bezeki's hideout. How I hoped to overcome the Djind and free five shadows, including Bell's.

As I finished up, he said, "You can count on me, Sean. When are we going to Upper Dry Fork?"

"Tonight, immediately," I said. "We don't have time to spare—"

But Buddy said: "No, not tonight."

"What do you mean, not tonight?" I said, not trying to hide the anger in my voice. "The clock is ticking away here."

Buddy held up his hands. "Okay, okay, give me a chance to explain, Sean. It will be dark shortly, and very cold. Pitch black and icy in those woods. We'd be lucky to find the shaft in those conditions. Then trying to set up in the freezing darkness? No, I recommend we wait at least until first light tomorrow...." He paused, then added: "Probably best to meet here about seven. I'll bring my granddaddy's old iron in my pickup. We can pick up the other stuff we'll need at the fire station, hardware store, and the service station on our way out of town. By the time we get to the Turner place it'll be starting to get light and a bit warmer." He waited for my response.

"I think he makes a good point about getting there after daybreak, Sean," Edel said.

Buddy knew the area well and understood the conditions this time of year. No doubt he was right. So, despite wanting to begin implementing the plan immediately, I nodded. But everyone could see my obvious distress.

Edel said, "Wise decision, Sean." Buddy nodded.

"According to the plan you've laid out, you don't want to get Junior involved or even alerted," Miss Dee Dee said.

I sucked in a deep breath, then said: "No, we don't. No law enforcement at this stage."

"Okay. Well...don't fret too much. I'll stay in contact with Doc Browning and his people in ICU while you're gone tomorrow morning. I'm sure Bell will be hanging tough, she's a trooper. You concentrate on what needs doing up there, Sean, you hear."

"I appreciate that, Miss Dee Dee."

"Okay," Edel said. "We meet here tomorrow morning, at seven?"

"Right," I said, wondering if I'd be able to get any rest tonight.

October 15, 2012—

We met about 6:55 the next morning at the *County Record* office, where Miss Dee Dee gave us a stoutly fortified mug of coffee and wished us luck. Buddy's grandfather's rusty iron stuff was in the bed of Buddy's truck.

We stopped at the hardware store, the fire station, and the service station to get everything else we needed.

We arrived at the Turner place a little after 7:30.

The woods were still dark and frosty as we hiked to where Miss Dee Dee thought the old mineshaft was located, but faint light was beginning to leak through the trees along the ridge to the east. Edel and Buddy were soon panting like sled dogs, because of their heavy fire-extinguisher backpacks. I had no pack, but I carried Grandpa's iron in one hand and a twelve-pound sledgehammer in the other. I, too, was soon huffing, puffing, and sweating, despite the morning chill.

We found the open shaft about 8:00, just as dawn began seriously encroaching into the lingering autumn darkness and chill.

Even before we reached the entrance, we could hear a small generator humming loudly.

It rested just inside the cave mouth, a thick extension cord disappearing into the darkness.

Good, I thought, the generator's sound will mask our preparations. I indicated a spot for the iron trap, about five feet outside the mouth of the entrance. Buddy, Edel, and I took turns pounding the long metal stake into the rock-hard ground, until we'd finally driven it deep enough to secure the trap. With an effort, the two other men pried apart the jagged teeth of the rusty bear trap and carefully laid it on the ground. We camouflaged it with forest debris, mostly golden leaves from the nearby sugar maples.

The jagged teeth of the trap were completely hidden, with the location marked by a blanket of yellow. The creature obviously hadn't heard our preparations. Good.

Now it was up to me. The dangerous part of the plan.

I stepped into the shaft's icy darkness and shivered. The tunnel cut steeply downward. Leaning back, I moved along, my heart thumping rapidly, my pulse racing wildly…comfortable movement stiffened by my fear.

Scared shitless, I had to stop and catch my breath.

I wasn't sure I could overcome my fear and carry on.

I closed my eyes, searching for some source of strength.

And that's when I heard Gramps in my head: *Sean, you have the heart of a Gaelic warrior—great CuChulain's blood races in your veins. Meditate, lad. Call on the Riastradh.*

I sucked in a deep breath, held it, concentrated, and peered into my inner darkness…and, after a few moments, there it was!

The burning white dot in the blackness.

I let my pent-up breath whoosh out, as if I were blowing up a balloon. The dot expanded, growing larger and larger, until it completely illuminated my inner darkness. A wave of energy washed through my body, across every neural synapse, until it reached the very tips of my nose, fingers, and toes.

The warm wave utterly relaxed me.

I blinked, my eyes fully adjusted to the shaft's darkness.

Without a trace of fear, I was calm, strong, and confident—energized in the firm grasp of the wasp spasm, ready to do battle with the ancient Djinn.

With my hyperacute vision, I followed the extension cord into the heart of darkness. Moving easily.

Until I was stopped by a plywood barricade that sealed off the shaft. The barrier was built around a small door and the refrigeration unit, with spackle and duct tape spread around liberally, sealing all the leaks in the wall.

Fearless, I did not hesitate but boldly hammered on the ice-cold door, shaking the whole barricade.

"Come out, Bezeki!" I shouted, the command echoing back up the narrow tunnel. "It is time for you to meet your master."

I stepped back several paces, steeled myself, and waited for about…five seconds.

The plywood barricade exploded, pieces of the door flying past my head.

Shadrach Black stood in the opening, his face an angry mask, his ancient black eyes peering at me, crazed and hateful.

He roared: "It's you, Gadjo!"

He moved toward me, supernaturally fast.

I waited for a fraction of a second, until his outstretched fingers almost touched my shoulders.

Then I turned and fled, not in a panic, but under complete control, luring the Djinn in my wake, just beyond his reach.

We sped up the steep incline.

Half way up, I heard him slip on loose debris and stumble. I slowed to glance over my shoulder....

A mistake, because at that moment his hand locked like a vise around my ankle.

Unfazed, I reacted, deftly twisting around whip-like and slamming my free foot into his chest, driving the air from his lungs. Breaking his grip on my ankle.

But the Djinn recovered rapidly and bounced to his feet, roaring defiantly, "Die!"

Again I fled.

My kick must have hurt him, though, because I could hear his labored breathing as we ran uphill, and I sensed him falling back.

So I slowed a bit, allowing him again to close the distance between us just as we neared the shaft entrance.

Bezeki was panting heavily now.

For a moment, I thought I could feel his wet breath on the back of my neck, which spurred me forward—

Bursting into the early morning light, I leapt over the pile of golden leaves like an Olympic hurdler.

Clank.

Hearing the metallic sound of iron teeth clanking shut, I stopped and turned.

"Ah-ooooogh!"

An angry, animal-like howl of pain shattered the forest silence.

The demon Bell and I knew as Shadrach Black was tugging violently at the jaws of the rusty bear trap, tight around his right ankle.

As the creature struggled mightily to free himself, throwing his weight to and fro at the end of the trap chain, Buddy and Edel moved closer from where they'd been hiding at the sides of the entrance.

Remaining out of reach of the crazed creature, they aimed and rapidly pumped their nozzles, dousing the monster from both sides with a steady stream of gasoline.

In moments, the air was filled with thick, pungent fumes.

The Djinn raged and howled, jerking back and forth, trying to escape and pull himself free, frantically uttering a stream of guttural Romany curses....

Buddy and Edel emptied both ten-gallon tanks.

"Look out!" shouted Edel as the Djinn broke the rusted chain securing the trap to the stake in the frozen ground, and then lunged in my direction. His clumsy effort was hampered by the massive trap locked around his foot.

Still entranced, I attacked, stepping inside and evading the Djinn's awkward attempt to claw at me. I dug a left hook into his throat. He straightened up, momentarily stunned. Giving me enough time to dig out of my pocket a can of lighter fluid and a Bic lighter.

Pointing the stem at the Djinn's heaving chest, only about two feet away, I squeezed out a steady stream of fluid, clicked the Bic and lit the flow.

A flamethrower!

Phoof!

The gasoline-soaked monster ignited with a loud *pop!*

Ha! I had brought the heat of the sun to Bezeki!

Instantly, the Djinn's hat, duster, and inner clothes were aflame. In the next second, I was driven back by the blistering heat.

The Djinn, though, stood locked in place, immobilized by the consuming flames gripping him in their fiery fingers—holding him in the center of a small sun.

Over the next few minutes, the demon-possessed shell of the Traveler, Shadrach Black, turned a leathery dark brown, blackened, blistered, and cracked apart in peeling strips, which were sloughed off...revealing the true physical nature of the ancient Djinn named Bezeki.

He was hairless, pale, slightly hunched-back, and short with long, heavily muscled arms. He looked nothing like his tall, thin, stooped-shouldered Shadrach Black disguise...except for those ancient ebony eyes peering hatefully from the fire-imprisoned creature.

In its final moments, the Babylonian Djinn uttered its last, hatefully derisive word: "Gadjos."

It disappeared from this world in a blinding nova of white light.

For a minute, a smoky remnant hovered over the rusty trap, like an ominous gray cloud. Then that last reminder of the ancient Djinn dissipated into the frosty morning air.

I blinked and breathed deeply, feeling shaky now, like the dying adrenaline rush after a boxing match.

Had I been truly in a state of Riastradh?

I couldn't be sure.

And who knew if I really possessed the mythical CuChulain's genes or not.

It didn't matter.

The three of us carried five frozen shadows out of the mineshaft into what a beautiful, sunny autumn day. As we were leaving the shaft, we torched what was left of Bezeki's hideout.

I sat in the back of Buddy's pickup with Bell's cold shadow resting across my lap, praying we'd rescued her spirit in time.

Dr. Browning met us at the hospital with a big smile. "She's in ICU, her vital signs climbing toward low normal. You want to see her for a few minutes?"

Teary-eyed, I could only nod.

I rushed to Bell's side and kissed her firmly on the mouth, then pushed her away. She was smiling and rosy-cheeked, but she still looked drawn and exhausted—she'd been in a long, draining fight for her life.

Choked up, I managed only, "Okay?"

"Yes, yes, I'm fine. But I'm not sure what happened to me after the grocery store. After I saw Shadrach Black pounce on my shadow."

I drank a glass of water, pulled myself together as much as possible, and then in a hoarse, proud voice, I explained how we'd brought the sun to Bezeki.

"He's permanently back in the bottle now!" Bell said, smiling broadly, after hearing it all.

I nodded and hugged her again. Thankful that we'd freed her shadow in time.

And then I glanced around, and noticed that the four other patients in the ICU were looking pretty chipper, too.

Chapter 15

Reclusive Carrier Dies in Fire

Junior McDowell reports that Hubert Jones, the carrier of the mysterious ailment affecting four youngsters from Upper Dry Fork, died in a fire October 14th. The reclusive Jones was squatting in an abandoned coal shaft on Upper Dry Fork and succumbed to a self-ignited fire in the tunnel. All four children he infected are doing well and will be released from Welch Community Hospital the first of next week. So, we can cross off the coal corporations as the villains this time. When asked for a last word, Junior McDowell stated that he wants to remind voters that he is again on the ballot in the November 6th election. The *County* Record supports Junior McDowell for Sheriff of McDowell County. Of course, he is running unopposed.

—*County Record,* October 21, 2012

October 30, 2012—

I re-read Miss Dee Dee's *County* Record wrap-up of the incident last night with a chuckle, especially the last line. Bell was recovering nicely, to the point where she was again assuming full management and supervisory responsibilities of our household…and me.

After I passed the forwarded copy of the *County Record* to her in bed, she read the article and said in a grateful voice, "Thank God, it's really all over now, Sean."

I said: "Yes, it is…."

And I truly believed that. But at the back of my mind there was a nagging doubt that I couldn't quite dispel. At the mineshaft, at the very end, when Bezeki was completely consumed by fire, there had been a final, glaring explosion of light. I'd blinked, cleared my vision, and stared at the empty bear trap.

Completely empty…not even a trace of ash.

The End

Gene O'Neill has seen five of his novels published and 140 short stories and novellas.

The shorter fiction has been published in five collections, including the retrospective, THE HITCHHIKING EFFECT. He has made the final ballot nine times for the Bram Stoker Award and taken the haunted house home twice. Currently he is readying the four book CAL WILD CHRONICLES for trade paperback publication, putting finishing touches on another novel, THE WHITE PLAGUE, and working on a novella collaboration with Chris Marrs, entitled ENTANGLED SOUL.

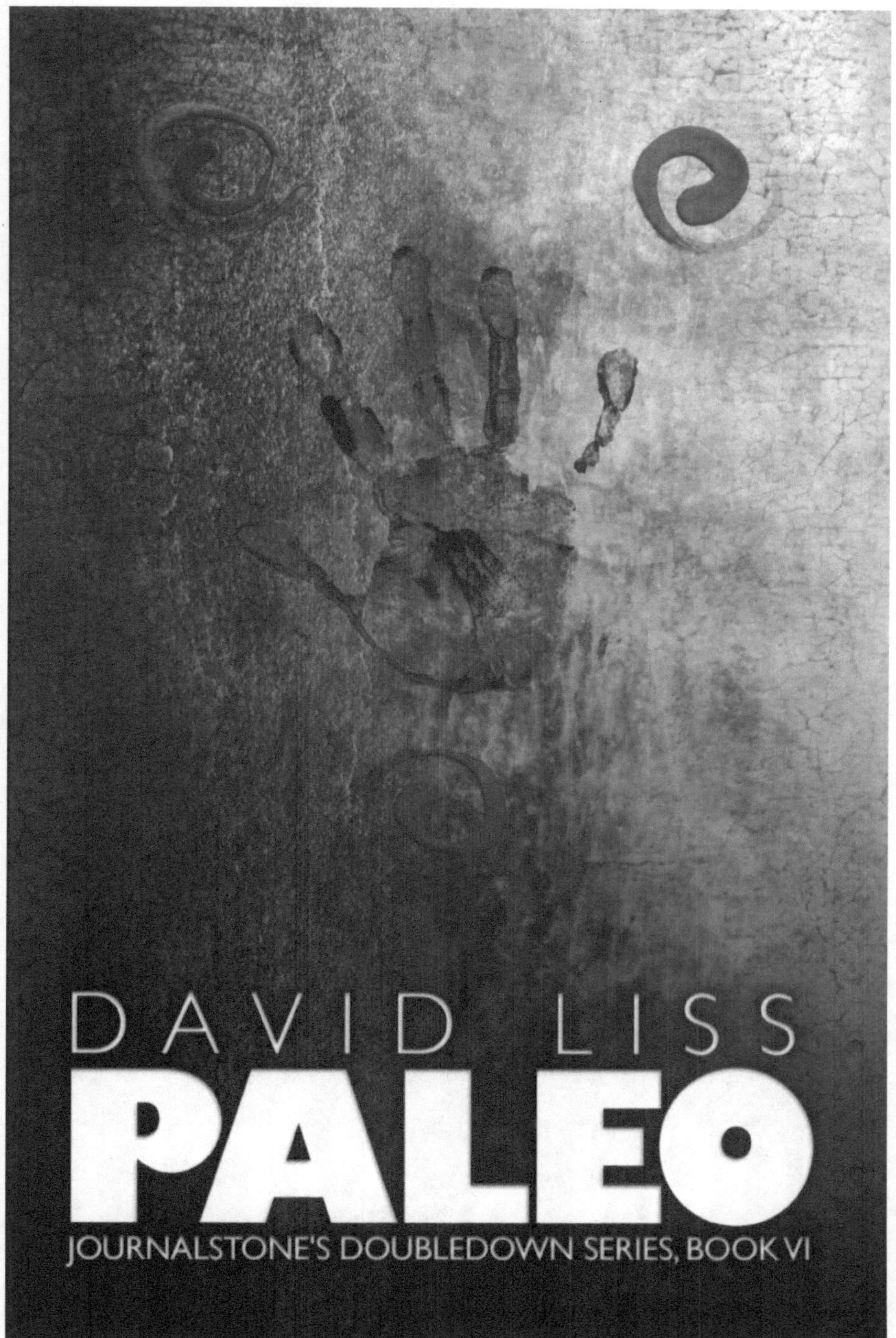

DAVID LISS
PALEO
JOURNALSTONE'S DOUBLEDOWN SERIES, BOOK VI

SOUL MATES

JOHN R. LITTLE

Wildwoman

By
Chris Marrs

JournalStone
San Francisco

JournalStone books may be ordered through booksellers or by contacting:

JournalStone
www.journalstone.com

ISBN: 978-1-942712-43-5 (sc)
ISBN: 978-1-942712-44-2 (ebook)

Library of Congress Control Number: 2015951509

Printed in the United States of America
JournalStone rev. date: September 11, 2015

Cover Design: Denis Daniel
Cover Art: M. Wayne Miller

Edited By: Dr. Michael R. Collings

Wildwoman

Chapter
1

1986

At the age of seven, Ghoulie Julie found a naked girl whose eyes were sewn shut.

Julie stalked the elusive unicorn through the forest. Another step and a shadowed form at rest came into view. *The unicorn.* Readying her imaginary net, she tiptoed toward it. *Careful. Careful. Don't startle it.* A bough creaked in the breeze. The figure took shape. Julie stopped.

A girl lay amidst the twigs and leaves scattered on the mossy floor. Her wide chest rose and fell in shallow breaths. Julie goggled at the broad shoulders, large hands, and gigantic feet. *Wow, I found a giant's kid.* The size difference made her feel even tinier than usual which, when compared to others her age, was already small. She crept a little closer. A fine down of auburn hair, the same shade as the giant's kid's long tangled tresses, covered her tanned body. Julie looked at her own pale skin, pockmarked with the weeping sores and blisters of eczema, then touched the recently shorn locks on her head. Her fingertips brushed against scabs. She studied the girl again and, despite her largeness, the flat nose, and square jaw, Julie found her beautiful. Maybe she'd want to be friends. No one else did.

"Wake up, girl," Julie said not quite brave enough to touch her.

The girl slept on. Julie clapped her hands and still nothing. Taking a deep breath, she snuck up, jiggled one big foot, and jumped back. When that didn't get a reaction, Julie put her hands on her hips and thought. *Ah, ha. The threads on her eyes. Maybe I need to cut them off.* Julie raced for home for scissors.

She breezed into her bedroom. Her Glo-Worm, once a prized possession, now a rare nighttime comfort, greeted her from its place on the pillow. Posters of *Rainbow Brite,* the *Carebears,* and *Strawberry Shortcake,* sprawled across the walls, but a new poster hung in the place of honor above her headboard. Her idol, *She-Ra: Princess of Power,* gazed into the room. Julie went to her desk and plucked the scissors from the tin-can pencil holder decorated with pictures of flowers and spiders.

Heading toward the door, a thought flitted through her mind. *Can't have a naked friend, it'd be too embarrassing.* So Julie rifled through the pile of clothes and blankets on the closet floor. At the bottom of the mess, she found an old white sheet with a hole cut in its center, a remnant from a costume for one of her games. *Perfect.* She pulled it out and snagged a belt that she never wore, then dashed out of the room, only to collide with her mom carrying an armload of dirty clothes.

"Slow down, Jules. There isn't anything so important that you have to run in the house." Her mom bent to pick up a fallen legwarmer, and, as she did so, Julie saw her mother focus on the scissors and sheet. "Where are you off to with those?"

"There's a naked girl in the forest with her eyes sewn shut, and she needs me to cut the thread so she can see." She held up the sheet. "And I'm going to give her a dress so she isn't naked anymore."

"Uh-huh, well you make sure to bring everything back inside when you're done playing with your imaginary friend."

"But…." *She wouldn't believe me anyway.*

"But what?"

"Nothing. See you later, love you, bye."

Her mom sighed, then said, "Be home for dinner."

Cedar trees towered over the scrub and brush, casting shifting mosaics of light and shadow across Julie as she knelt by the girl. Salt in the air mingled with the odor of a forest awakening from winter. An early mosquito teased her ear and drowned out the dim roar of waves throwing themselves against the distant cliff. She waved the bug away. *What if I cut the threads and she thinks I'm too ugly to be friends with?* Julie lifted the scissors.

She lowered them, gathered her courage, and raised them again. *Snip, snip, snip,* and the black strands over the left eye parted. She reached over and released the other one. The lids shot open, revealing a rich maroon with no iris or pupil. *Cool.* The girl flipped onto her side, stood, and ran into the woods.

"Come back!"

The giant didn't listen.

Dejected, Julie sat on the warm, damp, musty-smelling moss. *Stupid girl. I hope you get lost.* A lone gull screeched overhead as Julie stared at the place where the girl disappeared and, despite the rejection, willed her to return. A twig snapped, and a shadow loomed from behind. A hand gripped her shoulder. Julie jumped and twisted around. A boy jogged toward two others—baseball mitts dangling from hands—as three giggling girls came up the path and joined them. At the sight of her classmates, Julie's heart rolled, then pitter-pattered.

Go away. Leave me alone. Please.

"I touched Ghoulie Julie," Tyler said, raising his hand for high-fives.

"I'm not slapping your hand. It's full of Ghoulie Julie cooties," Danny said. The others mumbled in agreement and avoided Tyler's gaze.

Tyler scooped up a bat and ball from the ground. "You guys suck. None of you were brave enough to touch her."

"Or stupid enough, dummy," Colby said.

"You're a dummy," Tyler said.

"No, Ghoulie Julie's the dummy," Heather said.

Their attention shifted from Tyler to Julie. The sores on her face pulsed with heat from the blush spreading across her cheeks.

"Yeah, and she's ugly, too," Tyler said.

The game of *You're So Ugly* began. Julie knew fighting back wouldn't make them stop, so she went into herself and endured.

You're so ugly my dog wouldn't kiss you.

The handle of the scissors bit into the thumb and index finger of her hand and she wished it were She-Ra's Sword of Power.

You're so ugly your mom puts a paper bag over your head to talk to you.

She'd call on the power of the sword, transform into the beautiful warrior, and show them.

You're so ugly your parents wish you hadn't been born.

All dreams of turning into She-Ra disappeared as the taunt reminded her of the baby growing in her mom's belly. Julie's fear of being tossed aside when the baby came surfaced. She hugged her knees to her chest. Salty tears stung the lesions, and she hated the kids. The pack noticed that they had achieved their desired result and, laughing, went on their way. Their voices rebounded through the trees as they boasted about how they had made Ghoulie Julie cry. Gradually, the chatter faded.

Julie used the bottom of her sweater to wipe away moisture and snot, but her eyes kept leaking. A shaky sigh escaped. A random snippet of the girls' laughter echoed in the air and unleashed the anger continually simmering beneath. Hands clenched into fists, she stood, and stomped her feet in rage. *Not fair. Why did I have to be born ugly?* A branch cracked, and she froze, fearing the gang returned to tease her again. She left the sheet and belt where they lay and ran for home.

* * *

From behind the brush, a pair of maroon eyes watched her leave.

* * *

Spring blossomed into summer. Days grew warmer, nights shorter, and the final bell rang on the school year, releasing Julie from days of nine-to-three torture.

A *tap-tap-tap* on the window jolted Julie awake. The *Sci-Fi Choose-Your-Own Adventure* book slid off her chest and thunked onto the floor. The nightstand lamp cast a weak yellow glow in the dark room. Again the tapping came, hesitant and questioning. Mind muddled by sleep, Julie lay there, her heart pounding and bladder painfully full. She waited an entire minute, listening to the gentle patter of rain on the roof, nothing more. Relieved the tapping had stopped, she slipped out of bed and headed to the bathroom. Passing the window, she caught movement through the gap between the curtains. Two ovals of red light, the size of a small flashlight appeared to stare at her.

Julie stopped and strained to pick up the slightest sound. Shifting her weight from heels to toes and back, she debated whether to run or call for Dad. The scarlet ovals blinked. Julie cried out, and warm pee streamed down her legs. A guttural grunt came from the other side of the glass, then the crimson glow disappeared. *What was that? Was it real?* Too scared to move, she eyed the window, hoping the light wouldn't return and prove it existed outside her imagination.

Cold fabric pressing against her legs brought reality back. The acrid scent of pee embarrassed her—*stupid, you're not a baby*—and she stripped out of her pajama bottoms. In the cool air, the skin on her legs puckered and rippled, irritating the open sores. Using a dry bit of fabric from the pjs, she wiped herself down, clenching her teeth against the sting of pee on the rash. Julie shoved the pajama pants all the way to the bottom of her hamper. Not knowing what to do about the puddle on the carpet, she threw a dirty shirt over it, found fresh night clothes, and climbed back into bed. She huddled under the covers with her Glo Worm and waited for sleep. It was denied to her until the first morning birds sang and the soft glow of dawn touched the sky.

* * *

Grumpy and tired, Julie walked into a kitchen smelling of coffee and toast. Her dad sat behind an open newspaper while her mom cut a grapefruit into sections. A glass of orange juice and bowl of cereal waited on the plastic placemat marking Julie's spot.

"Good morning, sleepyhead," her mom said. "Eat up and go get dressed for dance class."

Julie flopped into her chair. "I don't want to go to dance class this summer."

"Really?" her mom said. Julie knew that tone; it meant guilt. "What would you rather be doing than taking classes and spending time with your mom at her studio?"

"I dunno. I just don't want to dance. I'm not that good at it anyway. Please, Mom, don't make me."

The newspaper ruffled and her dad cleared his throat.

"If you don't practice, you won't get better," her mom said. "Gary, help me out here."

Her dad folded the paper, set it on the table, and smoothed it down with a hand calloused from long hours spent felling trees in the bush. "I don't see why she can't have a break this summer, hon, if she promises to start again in the fall." He turned his attention to Julie. "What do you say, kiddo? You can skip the summer classes if you promise your mother you'll continue in the fall?"

"Yup," she said. "I promise."

The prospect of golden summer days spent in the forest opened up before her. She sat up straighter as prickles of excitement travelled up her spine and plans formed.

"And help your mother at the studio two days a week," her dad said. Then paused. "Since you can't be home alone, your mom will ask Mrs. Potts to stay with you." Julie saw her mom raise her eyebrows at that. "And I expect you to keep the house tidy and clean up after yourself."

Her enthusiasm diminished, and she slouched.

"Okay," she said.

He picked up the paper and hid behind it again before her mom could argue. The knife her mom was using clattered onto the table, and she stalked out of the kitchen.

"Thanks, Dad," Julie said.

"You're welcome, kiddo. And you're right, you're not a very good dancer. A bit of a disappointment to your mom, and you know she'll keep trying to make you into a dance star."

After breakfast, Julie dressed and headed out into the sunshine and her forest playground. She passed the back of the house and remembered the scary thing—dream—from last night. Convinced the rain tapping on the window had played tricks on her, she barely gave the window a second glance, but a smattering of wildflowers directly beneath it caught her attention. They looked like they'd been tossed into the air to land where they may. *A secret admirer?* The thought tickled her until she saw the huge footprints beneath the window and the fantasy morphed into disquiet. They were too big to be a boy's and why would a man be standing barefoot outside her window? She remembered the girl.

Julie backed away. The steady drip-drip of water plinking onto dirt beat in the background. She stopped. Steam rose from the wet grass as the sun warmed it. *What do I have to be afraid of?* On one hand, she really wanted the girl to be her friend, but she'd run away. On the other, who wanted to be friends with someone who snuck around at night to scare her? But what if the girl had brought the wildflowers? The gift decided it. Julie headed back to where she'd found the giant kid.

A large cedar basket—*big enough for me to climb into*—lay on its side at the entry of the clearing. With its woven cedar strips, the basket resembled pictures of the ones the Haida, northern west coast Native Americans, used to make. Julie had learned about them in school. She righted it by the strap and peered inside. Empty. A twig dug into her back as she looked at the canopy of boughs above. She sat up and scanned the area. The hairs on the back of her neck crawled. To the left, branches swished and leaves rustled as if someone or something had passed by. A spot of white came toward her from behind the greenery. Julie stood and tensed to run. The girl stepped out.

She wore the sheet, with the belt cinched at the waist. It looked like a mini-dress on her. While keeping an eerie maroon eye on Julie, she picked up the basket and slung it over her shoulder. They faced each other and, neither moving to leave, studied the other, then the girl smiled.

Julie called her Yani, and Yani called her Ulie. Together they built forts out of fallen cedar branches. The fragrant wood always made Julie sneeze, which would send Yani laughing in her deep, snorting way. They played hide-and-go-seek, battled ogres, and searched for fairies. When her parents smiled and said it was *nice* she had an imaginary playmate, Julie stopped telling them about Yani. Julie learned Yani didn't have friends either and, together, they felt normal.

She also learned not to touch Yani's ever-present cedar basket. The one time she did, it resulted in Yani throwing her to the ground and storming off with it. Julie didn't see her friend for two days after. When Yani returned, the girls acted as if nothing had happened.

* * *

Summer lazed its way toward fall.

Julie stared over the cliff to the sea below. Waves crashed against the rocks and tossed white plumes into the air to splinter into tatters by the wind. It ruffled her short hair and slipped through the thin fabric of her t-shirt. She shivered. The dirt-and-grass-stained hem of the dress flapped around Yani's legs, but, despite her scant clothing, she didn't seem bothered by the wind's bite. Julie tried to swallow away the ache in her throat and wished she'd thought to wear a jacket.

"Ulie," Yani said. "What's wrong?"

"School starts next week, and I don't want to go back, but you'll be there this year so maybe no one will bug me," she said.

Yani adjusted the cedar basket but didn't reply.

"You will be there, won't you?" Panic raced across Julie's nerves. She didn't want to be alone again.

"No."

Julie's stomach twisted at the possibility of going back to a classroom filled with jeers and taunts without Yani. She heard the name they called her whispering on the wind. *Ghoulie Julie*. Then something stung her shoulder—*ouch*.

She jumped back, madly brushing the spot where she'd been bitten. Another sting caught her on the back of the head. She looked to Yani for help, but she had disappeared. Crashing noises from the tree line made Julie turn to see the bullies striding into the clearing. The boys advanced while the girls hung back, smirking. Julie hunched her shoulders and lowered her head.

"Oooooh, look it's Ghoulie Julie. Don't jump," Heather said.

They laughed.

Julie ran.

"Get her!" Tyler said.

The boys raised their arms and let loose a barrage of rocks. They bounced around Julie, some managed to hit her. She sprinted into the forest. Branches thwacked her face and chest as she entered at full speed. She ducked under limbs, pivoted around trees, and vaulted over a moss-covered log, then her ankle rolled. Her leg buckled, and momentum tossed her face-first onto the forest floor. She slid, driving bits of leaves, dirt, and moss into her open sores, adding to the stabbing pain of her ankle. Discouraged, Julie lay there, each breath a controlled heave to hold back tears. A shadow stood over her.

"You okay?" Yani said.

"I'm fine. Go away," Julie said.

In the distance, but coming closer, she heard a boy call out, "Ghoulie Julie, where are you? Won't you come out and play with us?"

"Why won't they just leave me alone?"

"I know a place where they can't bother us."

Yani slid the shoulder straps off her arms and placed the cedar basket upright on the moss. The cracking branches, and the general cacophony of boys stomping through the forest, sounded nearer.

Yani opened the basket and said, "Quick, climb in."

"Sure, trap me. Like that'll stop them."

Yani's maroon eyes flared, changing the features from warm and friendly to scary, and Julie felt the blood drain from her face. Her breath hitched in a painful hiccough as, for the first time, Yani frightened her.

"Just do it."

Julie hesitated. Which would be worse, Yani or the bullies? Yani's eyes grew brighter. The noisy boys came closer. Julie looked in the direction of the boys then back to Yani and her scary eyes. Mind made up, Julie gulped, climbed into the basket, and fell into nothingness. She screamed without sound.

She landed on a dirt floor studded with pebbles that bit into her palms. Heart beating like a bird's, Julie sprung to her feet and tensed. She looked for Yani.

In the shadows of the dim light, Julie saw stalactites and rough rock walls of a large cavern, felt cool dampness on her skin. Water dripped somewhere in the dark. *Where is this place?* Yani landed on her feet beside her. The air shimmered and the basket appeared on the floor in front of them. Expecting Yani to turn on her, Julie flinched but Yani looked triumphant instead of cross. Her eyes having returned to the mellow maroon instead of glowing red.

When Yani began to speak, the words came out in grunts and hoots. Julie scrunched her nose and shook her head in confusion. *What's going on? Why can't I understand her?*

Yani frowned. She uttered something unintelligible, then spit on her palms and placed them over Julie's ears. Admittedly, a little weird. Next, she spit on her index finger and swiped it over Julie's lips.

Julie twisted her head away and said, "Gross. What'd you do that for?" Julie's eyes widened. The words in her head were English but the ones coming from her mouth sounded like Yani's guttural grunts and hoots. "How'd you do that?"

"Magic." She shrugged like it was no big deal.

"But how?"

"I don't know. I just do it. I couldn't show you before because my magic doesn't work in your world, just mine."

"Your world?"

"Yeah. Come see."

Yani took Julie's hand and led her to the mouth of the cave. Julie gasped.

Soft light cast everything from the trees to the blades of lush grass and wildflowers in a gentle golden-pink. Blossoms from a cherry tree—its trunk twisted with growths she wasn't quite able to make out—swirled in the breeze and landed in the creek winding its way through the orchard. In the creek bathed a couple. They were the largest adults Julie had ever seen. Sunlight played with the blue highlights in their long black hair as water

sluiced down the tanned skin of their naked bodies. Despite the couple's complete nudity, Julie couldn't keep from staring at them. *Their perfect.*

"That's my mom and dad," Yani said. She sighed, a heavy, sad sound.

"They're beautiful," Julie said.

The hand holding hers tightened, "I know."

Laughter reached the girls as Yani's parents playfully splashed each other. Julie wanted to stay in this apparently idyllic world forever.

"I don't want to go back," Julie said. "Can I live here with you? Please?"

"You want to stay with *me*?"

"Of course. We could be like sisters."

Yani opened her mouth to reply but frowned then sighed. Julie waited. Again, it appeared as if Yani was about to answer and, again, didn't. Julie barreled ahead instead.

"And Tyler and Heather and the rest of them wouldn't be able to pick on me anymore," she said.

Yani released Julie's hand and walked back into the dimness of the cave. Julie's heart broke a little at the idea that Yani was about to tell her "No." Disappointed, she made her way to Yani to try to change her mind.

"I don't live with my parents," Yani said.

At the unexpected reply, the pleas died on Julie's lips, and without thinking she said, "Why not?"

"Look at them and look at me."

"So. Look at me and my mom and dad, and they still let me live with them."

"It's different here."

"I don't get it. Where do you live then?"

"I'll show you."

Yani picked up her cedar basket, went to a narrow opening at the back of the cave, and disappeared. Julie slipped through it into a smaller cavern. The murky light of the larger cave gave way to sunlight streaming through a hole in the roof. Here, the walls were smoother and covered in crude pictures drawn in ash and

chalk. They depicted angry scenes of frowning people, battles, and beasts. A grass pallet lay along one wall, rows of shelves—laden with strange and wondrous-looking objects that Julie wanted to explore later—lined another wall, and a fire pit dominated the center. It seemed to Julie that Yani lived alone.

"Who takes care of you?"

"No one. I look after myself. But sometimes the witch Malika comes to give me food or keep me company." Yani led Julie to a wall-drawing of a young woman with yellow hair and purple, berry-juice eyes. "That's her."

"She doesn't look like a witch."

"Malika's not like the ones in your stories. She's nice."

Julie wasn't too keen on the idea of a witch for company, but if Yani trusted her, Julie guessed Malika was okay.

"Come on, Yani, please, please let me live here with you. We could take care of each other."

Yani tapped her lip with her finger then smiled.

"Okay. It'll be nice to not feel alone anymore."

Excitement zipped through Julie.

"Hallo, Daughter. Are you home?" A feminine voice, bordering on musical, called from the larger cavern.

Yani stiffened. "They never come in here."

"Your father and I just wanted to drop in and see if you're still alive," Yani's mom said.

A baritone chuckle echoed toward the girls.

Panic evident on Yani's face, she said, "They can't know you're here. Go back to your world and meet me tomorrow night at the cliff."

"Why can't I meet them?"

"You just can't. Quick, into the basket. It'll take you home."

"But if the basket comes with me, how will you get back?"

"It'll stay with me. Trust me." Trembling, Yani looked beyond Julie to the crevice. "Now go."

Yani's fear was contagious, and Julie caught it. Her knees wobbled as she climbed into the basket, then landed on the mossy floor of the forest, its dark greens and dirty browns jarring after the soft golds and pinks of Yani's world. She took a moment to

bask in the memory of the other landscape, then remembered Heather and the bullies. *Were they still looking for her?*

The waves crashed in the distance, a bird sang, but no sound of the bullies. Julie relaxed, and in doing so saw the purple-gray of twilight replacing the sunshine. How had it gotten so late? She'd only been gone a half hour or so, but maybe time worked differently there, more slowly.

Julie made her way home, part of her hoping her parents wouldn't notice she was late. Another part dreamed of the magic she'd could learn from Yani, dreamed of a life without bullies or baby usurpers. A life of being with an outcast like her.

* * *

Julie slammed the bedroom door.

Stupid mom, stupid grounding. I was only three hours late.

She kicked at the pile of clothes on the floor, then, as they scattered, remembered this was her last night at home.

Ha! That'll teach you to ground me. Bet you won't even miss me.

Julie planned what to take to Yani's, but the ache in her throat distracted her to the point that it felt like she'd swallowed barbed wire. The world swayed and her excitement drained away. Exhausted, she gave up, put on her pajamas, and, shivering, climbed into bed.

Sometime during the next afternoon, Julie surfaced from a fevered sleep to see her mom standing over her. A cold washcloth soothed her hot forehead. Julie tried to speak, to say she needed to get up, but the attempt set her throat on fire. Frustrated, she attempted to sit up. The room tilted and she groaned, which sent spikes through her throat.

"Shhh, sweetie, lie back and try to sleep," her mom said. She gently pushed Julie down and tucked in the covers. "I'll be in later to check on you."

Her mom went out into the hallway.

"How's she doing?" her dad said.

"She has a fever and sore throat. Looks like it might be strep again. If it doesn't clear up soon, I'll take her to the clinic."

In the jumbled mess of her fever-tainted mind, she thought, *I'm coming, Yani. Wait for me.* Then sleep drew her into its embrace, with disconnected dreams where beautiful people bathed in blood while children cried.

* * *

Autumn stars shone on Julie as she stood at the cliff waiting for Yani. She never came. Night after night, Julie snuck out to wait until, finally, she gave up and stopped coming. During those evenings, she never considered that Yani hadn't known about her strep throat or that Yani had returned many times looking for her, only to give up hope.

Chapter
2

1990

At the age of eleven, Ghoulie Julie's fear of her little sister, Clare, taking over was realized. Clare of the perfect skin and golden curls was a dance prodigy, something Julie could never be. Their mom let Julie quit dance and focused her attention on Clare. Just another reason to hate Clare and torment her at every chance. It also served to remind Julie she wasn't good enough for anyone. Not even Yani.

One night, after Julie's mom gave her heck for slamming a door in Clare's face, Julie snuck out and went to the cliff. She watched the clouds chase the moon while the ocean caressed the rocks below. She thought of Yani. As always, Julie willed Yani to remember her and come take her away. No one came.

Chapter 3

1993

At the age of fourteen, Ghoulie Julie came home on a cold fall day to find one of the logging company's trucks in the driveway. *Cool. Dad's home early for a change.* Feet freezing in her leaky boots, she stood in the foyer and heard a man's voice say, "No one saw the snag lying against the tree Gary was falling. I'm so sorry for your loss." Her mom wailed.

Julie rushed into the kitchen, dirty footprints in her wake, to see her mom and her dad's boss at the kitchen table. He awkwardly patted her mom's hand. They looked at her when she entered, and her mom jumped up to pull Julie into a tight embrace.

"There's been an accident," she said into Julie's hair.

The day of the funeral passed in a blur of perfumed ladies dressed in their Sunday best, ill-at-ease men, and a torrential downpour that sounded like the rain stick Colby had brought to school as it hit the open umbrella tops, coffin lid, and tarp covering the nearby pile of earth. Julie shifted in the metal folding chair and waited for her dad to pop up out of the coffin and tell them it was an elaborate joke.

Later that night, Julie crept out of the house to stand at the cliff. The deluge had stopped earlier, and the stars shone hard and cold around the full moon. Below, the waves committed violent suicide against the rocks, and Julie understood their pain. More than ever, she wished Yani would come back. When she didn't, Julie began to doubt Yani had even existed, started to believe her parents had been right in calling her an imaginary playmate. Slowly, the imaginative little girl inside her started to wither and die, and by the time Julie headed home, she had winked out. And with her, Yani.

Chapter 4

1996

At the age of seventeen, Ghoulie Julie witnessed the death of the sociopathic man who had terrorized the town by stealing three of its daughters. But before that, there was Clare.

Julie walked into a kitchen redolent with the spicy scent of curry underlain with the sweet note of coconut milk. Her mom stirred a pot on the stove while Clare set the table and hummed. Knowing she was supposed to help, Julie went to the cupboard and took out three glasses.

Her mom turned around, startled. "Oh, I didn't hear you come in. How were the twins? Did Mrs. Rooney finally pay you?"

"A handful as usual and, yes. Can we go to the mall and get our school stuff on Saturday?"

"Not this Saturday, it's the Summer Intensive Competition."

Oh, yeah—dance.

"Can you drop me off then? I'll walk to the theatre when I'm done."

"I can't see why not."

"But I want Julie to come to the competition." Clare bunched up her face in the way Julie knew preceded a tantrum. "She always brings me good luck."

Her mom set down the spoon and removed the pot from the stove before she said, "Sorry, Julie, your sister's right. We'll go to the mall next weekend. Oh, no we can't. Clare has a meeting with a potential sponsor."

Her mom's face took on a wistful expression at the mention of a sponsor, and Julie lost it.

"It's always about Clare with you isn't it. What about me? What about what I want?" Her cheeks burned with anger. "I'll bet you wish you only had perfect little Clare with her perfect skin and perfect dancing."

Her mom snapped out of the daydream. "Don't be so drastic. Clare works hard."

Julie gritted her teeth against the barrage of words she wanted to let loose but settled for banging the glasses onto the table. The last one cracked, and Julie stomped across the kitchen. Clare, eyes wide and shimmery with tears, stood in Julie's path.

"Get out of my way, brat," Julie said as she pushed Clare away.

Clare let out a squeak.

"Don't push your sister," her mom said.

Julie ignored the comment, charged into her bedroom, and slammed the door.

* * *

In her dream, Julie was seven again. Crouched in her closet, she listened to an unknown entity stalk the house.

"Ulie!" it called.

She huddled into a ball. *I'm not here.* The door to her room banged against the wall, and Julie jolted awake.

The early morning light cast everything in the washed-out grey tint of an old photograph. It took her a minute to register her bedroom door was open and slowly swinging to a stop.

"Is Clare in here?" her mom said from the doorway.

Julie grumbled and pulled the covers tighter. "Does it look like it?"

Her mom sighed in annoyance.

"Well, she's not in her room and I have to get her to the theatre in an hour."

"Not my problem."

Julie rolled over to go back to sleep.

"Enough with the sass, young lady. Get up and help me look for her. I don't want her to be late. It's competition day, remember?"

"I remember wanting to go to the mall."

"Just come help."

Julie tossed back the blankets. The chilly air raised goose bumps and helped clear her mind of the sleep-webs.

"I don't see why I have to. It's not like it's a big house," she said.

"Her window's open so I want you to look in your old fort. Lord knows why she goes out the window when there's a perfectly good door."

Yeah, when she does it, it's okay, but if I did, I'd get crap. Julie never voiced those thoughts. Experience had taught her Clare was untouchable. She pulled on a sweater, laced up her sneakers, and went to search for her sister.

Grey clouds roiled across the sky as the wind teased them into a fury. The air smelled damp with impending rain and wrapped Julie in its clammy embrace. She shivered and crossed her arms as she walked through a morning more like fall than summer. When she reached the fort, she poked her head inside. No Clare. *Great, now I'm going to be blamed for her not being here.* She snorted and went back to the house.

As she passed by Clare's open window, a green shape on the grass brought her to a halt. Her old Glo-Worm, now Clare's, lay there, its plastic head smeared with dirt. Julie bent to pick it up and noticed footprints. Two sets, one small and one large. The blood rushed from her head and, dizzy, she dropped to her knees.

"Mom!" she said. No answer. Panic tore at her chest. "Mom! Get out here!"

Crashing sounds came from inside Clare's room, then her mom stuck her head out the window.

"What is it? Did you find her?"

Julie showed her the toy.

"There are footprints, too." Her voice cracked.

"I don't understand what you're getting at. Of course, there are footprints. Did you check the fort?"

"There are two sets of prints." She started to cry.

Her mom gave a strangled moan and disappeared into the room. Julie could hear her repeating, "Not Clare. No, not Clare."

After her mom called 911, she huddled with Julie on the couch while cops stomped in and out of the house. A thin reedy man in plain clothes stopped in front of them.

"Is there any reason for Clare to have run away?" he said.

"Of course not. She's nine," her mom said. Julie felt her tense. "Oh God, you don't think…those other girls…"

Her mom buried her head in Julie's shoulder and wept. Feeling like the responsible adult instead of a child, Julie patted her mom's back and whispered they'd find Clare soon. She didn't believe it. Julie held her mom tighter.

* * *

The summer marched its way into a proper fall. With each passing day, Julie's mom lost a little more hope and took to staying late at the studio. Julie retreated into an angry combination of loss and resentment. The start of the school year ushered in its own set of problems.

Mr. Dean—the secret fantasy crush of most of the girls in his class—finished reading Coleridge's *The Rime of the Ancient Mariner*, closed the textbook, and set it on his desk. He turned to face the class.

"So, can anyone tell me what they think might have been the significance of the albatross?"

Kids coughed, a chair scraped along the floor, and papers rustled, yet Julie paid no attention to any of it, including Mr. Dean's question. In her imagination, Mr. Dreamy Dean confessed his love for her, said he didn't care how she looked because she had inner beauty. He got down on one knee and asked if she'd marry him.

"What's your answer, Julie?"

"Yes, I'll marry you."

Laughter brought her back to reality. Everyone stared at her as Mr. Dean watched her, clearly annoyed. Ears burning, Julie lowered her eyes. She heard Tyler and Danny whisper and chuckle.

Mr. Dean shot a warning glance at the boys, then said, "Not quite the answer I was looking for. I suggest you start paying attention."

More tittering, this time from the girls in the back of the room. Julie was thankful that before things became worse, the bell rang, and books slammed shut as the class prepared to leave.

Above the noise, Mr. Dean said, "Your homework tonight will be to write a five-hundred-word essay on Coleridge's use of the albatross as metaphor."

Julie scooted out of her chair, fairly ran out the door, and started for her locker. Fighting against the tide of teenagers, she hugged the wall. Someone mentioned Clare's name, another whispered *Ghoulie Julie,* but instead of checking to see who spoke, she bowed her head and almost missed seeing Heather and her entourage striding down the center of the hallway. Manicured fingers gestured and flicked long hair out of eyes. The girls' giggles rose above the din of shutting lockers, and more than a few boys stopped to gaze at them. Julie slipped into the restroom to wait until they passed.

I so do not need to deal with them today. Julie clenched her fists and prayed they hadn't seen her. Only the second week of school, and already she had to dodge the group. Their voices grew louder.

"Hold up. I need to pee first," Heather said.

Julie darted into a stall, put her books on the back of the toilet, and climbed onto the seat. The empty room exploded into a cacophony of meaningless teenage babble and effervescence. Other groups of giggling teens had followed Heather in. *Lovely.* Julie crouched and hoped she wouldn't fall in while waiting for everyone to leave, especially Heather. Hating herself but not able to stop, she worried a scab on her forearm until blood oozed around the edges. She licked her finger—salt and copper—and pressed it against the wound.

The wispy sound of perfume being sprayed followed a pause in conversation. Julie's nose tickled when the sweet, cloying scent reached it. She imagined what would happen if they discovered her hiding in the stall and plugged her nose. *Oh God, no, no, don't sneeze.* The toilet in the next cubicle flushed and the door crashed shut.

"Whew, who's going hootchie with the perfume?" Heather said. "It's enough to gag a maggot."

The bubbly atmosphere vanished and the girls laughed, a nervous twittering like birds unsure if a predator is present or not.

"Sorry," a meek voice answered. Julie didn't think the poor girl was a part of Heather's group.

Julie could almost feel the wariness in the air. Heather huffed and banged what Julie assumed to be her purse onto the counter top. Water ran, then stopped. The paper-towel dispenser clunked in the absence of chatter, then the third-period bell rang. The atmosphere relaxed, and, yakking away again, the most of the girls departed.

"Did you guys hear what Ghoulie Julie said in English?" Heather said.

Sneeze forgotten, Julie felt her cheeks pale.

"Dan told us," Trisha said. "What a loser."

"I'll bet even in her imagination Mr. Dreamy Dean would run away screaming," Mandy said.

The sound of their laughter echoed like hyenas on the hunt. Julie put her chin in her hands to wait them out while she tried not to cry.

"She's so weird, I'll bet she had something to do with her little sister…" the closing door cut off the rest of Heather's words.

Heart heavy with the knowledge her senior year would be more of the same old story, Julie climbed off the toilet seat and retrieved her books. She slunk out of the restroom and into the deserted hall. Her flats clicked in time with her slow steps but grew louder when she picked up the pace. *Low blow to mention Clare, even for Heather.* She started to run, her flats clattering against the linoleum. At the end of the hall, she rammed the metal handle of the door and burst into the autumn sunshine.

She ran, hard and fast, with no particular direction in mind, only the need to get away from the school, Heather and her groupies, from everyone. The asphalt sent little jolts of pain up her legs. Flats weren't designed for running, but ditching school wasn't something she'd planned on while choosing footwear that morning. A smidge of remorse tugged at her. She'd never before skipped school. A car passed, the brake lights briefly flashing before it sped off. Its appearance made her feel exposed, so she veered off the road and into the woods.

It didn't take long to locate the deer path that ended at the cliffs. She counted herself lucky she'd instinctively turned left out of the school parking lot. Left led toward home while right would've taken her into the town of Cressidia.

Cressidia couldn't be called a town or a city but something in-between. It combined some of the trendier amenities of a larger city with a small-town atmosphere. If the residents yearned for big-city experiences, Seattle lay two hours in one direction and Portland in the other. Surrounded by forest and bordered by the ocean, Cressidia was initially supported by the forest and fishing industries. Over time, people settled there for its seclusion and beauty, and, slowly, tourists discovered it as well.

While Julie walked, sunbeams filtered through the canopy of boughs. The early fall light edged the trees in gold and cast spotlights of the same hue on the ground. Twigs snapped underfoot.

She worried. Did the school realize she was gone yet? Would they call her mom? Another thought rushed in and brought its friend, guilt. *Clare and the missing girls. Oh no, will Mom think I've been taken, too?* Something crashed through the brush to her right, and she stopped.

Something moved behind her, and she whirled around. Nothing. Branches snapped to the left. A dark shape whipped around a tree trunk. Perhaps thinking about Clare had managed to whistle up her captor. Julie's heartbeats doubled and her muscles locked. The form broke cover and ran at her. Julie dropped her textbooks and bolted.

Panicked breaths drowned out any sound of pursuit, but she expected a hand to grab her shoulder at any moment. The path swerved to the right. She flailed her arms in a feeble attempt to remain upright as her flats skidded along loose pebbles. For a second, she thought gravity would win, but she stopped the slide.

Julie brushed a lock of hair off her sweaty cheek and hazarded a glance over her shoulder. A tall, husky figure stood in the middle of the path. There was something familiar about the slouched stance, and Julie slowed. The breeze stirred the trees, allowing a momentary shaft of sunlight to illuminate the form. Disjointed images of a square face and auburn hair covering head, body, arms, and legs flashed in Julie's mind. Maroon eyes blazed. *No, she's not real. I'm seeing her because I don't want to see the true face of the kidnapper.* She took off again.

"Ulie, come back," Yani said.

I did not just hear that.

A little farther ahead, the path doubled on itself. Almost home. In case the kidnapper followed her, she added more speed. Soon the woods thinned and she sprinted into her backyard. Leg muscles quivering and lungs burning, she raced to the side door, lifted the mat, and retrieved the key. It rattled against the lock—*come on, damn it*—before sliding in. Once inside, she slammed the door, bolted it, and leaned against the chilly wood to catch her breath. Paranoia pushed her away from the door. She tore through the house to check that the windows were locked, all the while denying the vision of her childhood imaginary friend.

Sweat soaked the underarms of her t-shirt and dripped down her torso. It began to cool and gave her something else to focus on, a shower. If she didn't get one soon, the salty residue would exacerbate her eczema and drive her insane with itching. After confirming all windows were locked, she grabbed her robe and headed to the bathroom to let the hot spray wash away the sweat and the ugly day.

Later, relaxed, she left the room, a plume of lavender scented steam billowing out with her. Lavender, not her favorite smell, but the only scented soap that didn't bother her skin nor make the sores spread. Although puberty had cleared her face and stomach of the bothersome affliction, her arms, legs, and back still broke out in varying degrees. She pulled the belt on her robe tight and tucked the end of the towel covering her hair under the collar.

The smell of overripe banana pervaded the air in the kitchen, and the linoleum felt cool under her heat-reddened feet. She went to the fridge for a snack and saw the scribbled note tacked to it.

Julie,

I won't be home until after dinner. There's lasagna in the fridge. Around 4:00, please put it in the oven at 180°. Thanks.

Mom

Not surprised her mom chose to stay late at the studio, Julie looked at the clock on the stove—only quarter to one, lots of time to read. She wandered into the living room. The Stephen King novel she'd started lay on the back of the secondhand couch. Perfect. She picked it up and headed to her room to lose herself in the book.

"Julie Marie!" her mom said. "Get your butt into the kitchen."

The yelling yanked Julie out of the world of a teenage girl with telekinetic powers, an ability Julie coveted. She cringed at the use of her middle name, never a good sign, and figured her mom knew about the ditching. But the clock on the nightstand showed it was nearing seven, too late for her mom to have found out.

"Did you hear me, young lady?"

Julie closed the book and, without some trepidation, got up.

The comforting aromas of warm tomato sauce and hot cheese enveloped Julie when she entered the kitchen. But her mom's cocked hips cocked and crossed arms spoke the opposite of comfort. *Uh, oh.*

"Why did you leave school today?" She tapped her bicep with her index finger.

Julie gazed around the room, looking everywhere but at her mom.

"I'm waiting."

Because everyone hates me and thinks I'm ugly, and I have no friends, was what she wanted to say but couldn't speak the words. They wouldn't have any impact, anyway; her mom never believed her when Julie confided in her. Julie balled her hands into shaking fists. Knowing she couldn't speak the truth infuriated her.

"Because I felt like it," she said instead.

"Not a good enough answer, Julie."

"It'll have to be because it's true." *Wait a minute, no one called here so how did she find out I skipped?*

Before Julie gave voice to her internal question, her mom answered it. "Do you know how worried I was when the school called the studio? Not to mention just a little embarrassed to have to interrupt my meeting with the costumer?"

"Yeah, you were so worried you rushed home. Nice, Mom." She clenched her fists harder. The trembling increased and traveled up her arms to settle in her shoulders. "Did it cross your mind I might have been kidnapped like Clare?"

The expression on her mom's face flashed from angry to sad to hurt and back to angry. "Don't be silly. You're too old."

A strangled scream of frustration tore at her throat. She turned on her heels and stormed out of the room.

"And don't say she's been kidnapped. We don't know that," her mom said. "She might show up at any moment."

Julie flung herself onto her bed and buried her face in the pillow. Deep sobs wracked her body as her mom stood on the other side of the door and demanded that they talk. Knowing her mom wouldn't come in, Julie ignored the command. There was nothing to talk about; her mom had made it clear how important Julie was. Soon the torrent slowed to sniffles, then a random hiccough, before completely stopping. Swiping mucus and tears from her face with the sleeve of the robe, Julie resigned herself to being truly alone.

Once upon a time, before Clare and before the death of their dad, she had had a family.

Now, no one.

* * *

Fall waltzed toward winter. Another girl went missing and displaced Clare as the featured attraction. It caused a renewed uproar within the community, and, while the police had made no arrests, they followed up on several suspects. The Winter Formal loomed, and the preparations gave the students something to keep their minds off the missing children.

The barren maple trees rattled their branches in the wind, sounding like the scrape of bone on bone. Julie shivered, zipped her coat higher, and pulled her hat over her chilled ears. A small knot of teens strolled ahead of her, laughing and chatting. In her mind, she walked with them, joined in their conversation, shared the warmth of friendship. But the wind tore the illusion to pieces by stealing their words.

At school, she crinkled her nose at the scent of burning furnace oil as heat hit her face and hands, making her nose run and fingertips tingle. A scan for Heather and her entourage revealed a mostly empty hallway. She made for her locker. Glittery posters for the upcoming Winter Formal dotted the walls to mock and remind her of a life never to be hers.

During lunch hour, Julie sat, as usual, at the empty table along the back wall. Trays banged; boys shouted to each other from across the room. The smell of fried food mixed with the odor of too many teens in one place, making it hard to eat. Julie listlessly pushed a congealed mass of macaroni and cheese around her plate while daydreaming of the future. *One day, determined to make this idiotic school and loser town part of her past, she would become a successful psychologist. Surrounded by tons of friends, with a handsome husband to escort her to all the exclusive parties.* But not today.

"Julie," Heather said.

Julie jumped. Heather, her boyfriend Tyler, and the rest of Heather's entourage stood around her. *Heather never calls me just "Julie."* Anxiety stole the saliva from her mouth and pushed her stomach into her feet. Being called just *"Julie"* couldn't bode well for her.

"I'm sorry I've been a bitch to you all these years."

Julie squinted at Heather and tried to figure out her angle while waiting for the taunts and jokes to start.

"Look, I'm really sorry about Clare and what happened. It's our last year here and I was hoping we could put the past in the past and try to be friends," Heather said. "We all do. Don't we?"

Tyler and her groupies nodded, muttering random apologies. Julie didn't buy it; she knew Heather better than that. The girl thrived on making people feel small. Besides, one apology wasn't going to make up for years of torment. Without replying, Julie tossed her wadded napkin onto the plate and moved to leave. Heather blocked the way.

"Look, I'm serious, I don't want it to be like this anymore. You actually seem pretty cool."

Now Julie knew Heather was up to something—no one thought her *cool*.

"Um, excuse me, I have to go," she said and tried to get around Heather.

Heather studied Julie for a moment then said, "I get your hesitation, but why don't you come with us to *The Bean Grinder* after school today and see if I'm not telling the truth."

The Bean Grinder was the new trendy coffee shop where all the popular, and the bravest of the not-so-popular, kids hung out, just three doors down from her mom's dance studio. Julie passed it almost every day and yearned to go inside. She had never had the courage. Now, she was being invited. The small voice in her head warned against going, but the friendless part that craved acceptance told the voice to shut up.

"Okay, I'll go." The little voice groaned while her heart cheered.

"Alright. Meet us on the front steps after school. Colby's driving," Heather said.

Julie's mind stalled upon hearing Colby was driving, she blushed and hoped the others didn't know why. Then Heather and her friends walked away, leaving Julie to stare at their retreating backs and wonder if the new life she craved had begun. Or if she had just made a huge mistake?

Expecting them to turn on her, ridicule her in class for accepting a faux invitation, she was pleasantly surprised when Trisha asked to sit next to her in Biology. And after school, it astonished her to find the group already waiting on the steps. Maybe, just maybe, this was her year.

Colby parked his dad's van, and the girls tumbled out in a crush of chuckles and perfume. Julie, the last to exit the vehicle, stepped onto the sidewalk and marveled at the switch in and group's attitude.

A few minutes later, smiling, she followed them into *The Bean Grinder*.

They smelled the earthy yet bittersweet aroma of the shop and heard the cries of a baby and the whoosh of milk forced through the steamer. After a terrifying moment of not knowing what half the items on the menu were, Julie decided on the hot-chocolate-and-coffee combination, café mocha. It sounded the least complicated.

Tyler and Danny had arrived before them and secured a table near the back. Once everyone received their drinks, they threaded the gauntlet of tables to join the two boys. Tyler frowned at seeing Julie, but Heather poked him in the ribs, then whispered in his ear. Julie pretended not to notice and sat in the chair against the wall.

Although the others jumped into their customary chatting and teasing, Julie didn't feel left out. Every once in a while she'd toss in a comment but was more content to watch, listen, and sneak peeks at Colby. She learned that Heather didn't get along with her mom, that Colby lived with his dad while his mom lived in Portland, that Trisha smoked, and that Tyler's dad owned the strip mall on the way out of town.

"You know, you might look good if you put on some makeup once in a while," Heather said. All eyes turned Julie's way—*uh oh, here it comes*—and her guard went up. "You have a pretty face."

Not quite the comment she expected.

"A little mascara, some eyeliner, and a bit of lip gloss…What do you think girls?"

Mandy, who'd sat slumped in the chair, perked up and said, "Ooooh, a makeover. I like it."

"I don't know," Julie said fiddling with her near-empty cup, debating whether to tell them that makeup might irritate her skin.

"It'll be fun," Heather said. "You *do* want to hang with us don't you?"

The ultimatum hovered between them. *Here's your chance to gracefully disentangle yourself from them,* the rational part of her said. *But you'll be alone again and you don't want that,* the loneliness chimed in. No, she definitely didn't want to be by herself again, no matter how tenuous Heather's offer of friendship may be.

"Okay, why not?"

Heather clapped her hands. "Alright then." She gave Julie a once over. "And we'll have to do something about your clothes. Friday we'll hit the mall, and Saturday, we girls will sleepover at my house. Does that work for everyone?"

"Works for me," Trisha said.

"Me, too," Mandy and Monika said together then said, "Jinx." They laughed and swatted at each other.

"Julie?" Heather said.

A small part still wanted to say *no* but she said, "Yup, me too."

The brakes on the van squealed when Colby guided it to a stop in front of Julie's. Last to be dropped off, she had been too nervous to talk so the ride had been silent. When Julie fumbled with the door latch, Colby reached over and popped it open for her. His arm brushed against her chest. The contact tingled and made her ears turn red. Hoping he wouldn't see her swoony expression, she scooted out of the van.

"Thanks for the ride."

"No prob." He shifted the vehicle into reverse.

She shut the door and waved. Julie floated into the house on a cloud of happiness, thoughts of Colby's arm on her chest, sleepovers and makeovers whirling around her mind. For the first time, she felt normal.

* * *

From the brush at the side of the house, a pair of glowing red eyes narrowed.

* * *

Julie pushed the doorbell. Her overnight bag slung over one shoulder, she turned to watch the traffic pass. She couldn't believe she stood here on the stoop, about to spend the night at Heather's. Come last Monday, Julie had anticipated a return to the way things had always been. She had even spent the first half of the morning dodging Heather and her entourage, but they caught up with her during a class change. Instead of ridiculing her, as usual, they chatted with her, compared weekends, then invited her to sit at their lunch table. The rest of the week had passed in joyous camaraderie, and Julie had never been happier.

Footsteps padded toward the door. It opened, and Heather's mom ushered her in.

Julie stood on a beige mat and took off her shoes. The sounds of a video game blared through the sage-green and butter-yellow foyer. A set of stairs on the right led to the upper level.

"The girls are upstairs in Heather's room. Go on up." Julie hesitated as Heather's mom began to walk away. "Last door on the right."

"Thanks."

Heather's mom flapped a hand and kept walking, then stopped in front of the entrance to another room. "Turn down that game. Damien? Do you hear me?"

Julie didn't wait to find out whether he lowered the volume, instead she bounded up the stairs. Eggshell-blue walls led her down a hallway devoid of anything to suggest a family lived here. No little tables of knick-knacks or pictures on the walls, only the sterile span of blue. She knocked on Heather's door.

"Go away," Heather said.

Julie cringed and almost left but took a deep breath and said, "Um, it's me. Julie."

A flurry of noise came from the other side of the door before it opened, and Heather pulled her into a tidy room lit by candles. Mandy, Trisha, and Monika sat in a row on the bed, looking as though they were hiding something. Their guilty expressions gave Julie pause.

"Sorry, I thought you were my mom." Heather shut the door.

"What's with the candles?"

The girls looked from one to the other like they were communicating via telepathy. At the same time, they turned back to Julie. Their action brought to mind *The Stepford Wives,* a novel she'd read last summer and found eerie.

"Trisha brought her Ouija board and we're trying to contact spirits," Monika said.

Goosebumps rippled along Julie's arms and puckered her scabs. She rubbed her biceps in an attempt to smooth the bumps, lest the girls see and think her afraid.

Heather nudged Mandy and said, "Move over and let Julie in and we'll try again."

They rearranged themselves into a loose circle around the Ouija board resting on Heather's queen-size bed. Cautious, Julie sat cross-legged and placed her fingertips on the planchette with the others. This didn't feel right, and she considered bringing up the reason for the sleepover, her makeover. But the others seemed intensely focused on the board so she dropped the idea for the moment.

"Now what?" she said.

"Quiet, let me ask it a question." Heather scowled. Julie clamped her lips together. "Is anyone there?"

The planchette wobbled and moved to *yes*.

A soft *oh* escaped Trisha, then she whispered, "It didn't move before."

"Ask it my name," Mandy said. "So we know it's for real."

"What is the name of the girl sitting across from me?" Heather said.

They watched as the planchette spelled out *M-a-n-d-y*.

"Someone's moving it," Mandy said, her face paling. "It didn't move until Julie got here."

The girls gazed at Julie, a strange mix of fear and curiosity flashing across their features.

A knot formed in her stomach. *Are they going to gang up on me now?*

"I'm not doing it," she said. "Really, I'm not."

The following pause lingered a little too long and pulled the knot tighter.

"I believe her," Trisha said. The ball in Julie's stomach dissipated. "Ask something else."

After a slight pause, Heather said, "Who has a crush on me?"

The planchette dragged its way across the board to spell *T-y-l-e-r*.

"That's like cheating," Mandy said. "He's your boyfriend."

"Okay, then, who has a crush on Mandy?" Heather said.

P-a-t.

Mandy rolled her eyes and said, "Not that skinny little geek in math class."

It wasn't intended as a question for the board, but the pointer whipped to *yes*.

Everyone laughed and teased Mandy, even Julie. It felt good to mock someone else instead of be mocked.

"Enough ladies," Heather said. She cast a sideways glance at Julie. "Who has a crush on Julie?"

Julie held her breath, dreading the answer *No one* while secretly hoping it would name someone. The planchette spelled out *C-o-l-b-y*.

"Bullshit," Julie said then blushed. "You guys moved it this time."

"No, it's true," Heather said. "He told Tyler after that day at The Bean Grinder and Tyler told me. Colby's shy, though."

Julie didn't know what to say so said nothing as her heart swelled and her stomach fluttered.

Monika broke the silence. "Let's try contacting the dead kids."

Julie studied her lap. "Please, let's not."

"I'm not sure that's a good idea. You know...," Mandy said and tipped her head toward Julie. "Anyway, how do you know they're dead?"

"We don't. I'll ask," Heather said. The girls placed their fingertips onto the planchette. Julie hesitated, then joined in. "Are the missing kids dead?"

"Way to be blunt," Monika said.

Julie intently watched as the pointer moved to *yes* and her inner world cracked. It slid to *no,* then back and forth between the two before stopping in the middle of the board. Mandy giggled nervously.

"Well, that was helpful," Mandy said.

"Can we stop now?" Julie said. "It doesn't know."

Heather shot her a glare. "Do you know who took the kids?"

Yes.

The flickering flames flared, eliciting a collective gasp. The girls' shadows dancing along the wall darkened, became almost menacing, and a sense of tense anticipation thickened the air. Julie leaned closer toward the board.

"Who is it?" Heather said.

*U-l-i-*e, then *k-n....*

Julie scrambled backward until the rail of the headboard dug into her back. The pointer slipped off the board. Her mind whirled around the first four letters, trying to deny them. No one except her old imaginary playmate had ever called her *Ulie. How would the board know?* She could only assume that the board was going to spell *knows* next, but Julie had no inkling as to who the kidnapper was. Why would the planchette say she did? *It's only a silly game, means nothing.*

Monika smacked Julie's leg. "Lame-o, what'd you do that for?"

Heart beating a painful tempo in her chest, Julie found solace in the pattern on the bedspread and contemplated the best way to answer.

"Because it's lying. It doesn't know who has Clare. I mean, what kind of name is *Uliekn* anyway?" Julie said.

At the mention of Clare, the girls looked everywhere but at Julie.

"Who knows what it was trying to spell. You didn't let it finish," Heather said. "Come on, let's ask again."

"Count me out," Julie said. "I don't think I really want to know."

"I'm bailing, too," Mandy said. She leaned against the wall. "This is getting too creepy for me."

"Whatever," Heather said.

Julie heard the sneer in Heather's tone. Monika and Trisha shuffled to make the broken circle a triangle. Before Heather could repeat her question, a knock on the bedroom door startled them. The knob turned. Heather grabbed a pillow and covered the Ouija board as her mom stuck her head inside the room.

"Pizza's here," her mom said. "Come down and eat."

"We'll be out in a minute, Mom," Heather said. "Can we eat in here?"

"If you promise you won't get pizza sauce on everything?"

Heather rolled her eyes. "Of course. We're not four."

"Don't roll your eyes at me, missy. And blow out those candles before you head downstairs." Her mom left without shutting the door.

By the time they came back to Heather's room with plates of pizza, the Ouija board and its messages were forgotten. The rest of the night passed in a fit of giggles, gossip, and remaking Julie. When they finished with her, she didn't recognize herself. For once, she didn't hate her appearance, thought she might almost be pretty.

* * *

Condensation misted the windows of The Bean Grinder. Julie wiped a spot clear with the sleeve of her sweater and watched the rain bounce on the sidewalk, all the while keeping an eye out for Colby. A shredded napkin lay beside her coffee cup and, forearms leaning on the edge of the table, she tore another into strips. Her leg jittered up and down as she wondered where he was, whether he would even show. A glance at her watch told her it was a half hour past the time they were to meet. She blew a strand of hair out of her mascaraed eye, peeked out the window, then decided to give him another fifteen minutes. Deep down she worried his invitation had been peer pressure from the group, that he didn't really want a coffee date with her.

The door opened, letting the cold wind in. It swirled the newspapers on the stand, and when they settled, Julie saw a family of three standing there. Not Colby. Then he ducked out from behind them, waved, and made his way over. Julie crumpled the napkin she'd been ripping and dropped it into her lap. Her stomach flip-flopped as her breath caught.

He came.

"Sorry I'm late. I promised Danny I'd drop him off at work after school, and he took his sweet-ass time."

"No worries."

He checked out the short line, then said, "I'll be right back. You want something?"

"No, I'm good, thanks. If I have any more coffee I'll get the shakes."

Julie watched him join the queue, still not believing how suddenly her world had changed. For years, she'd been Ghoulie Julie; this new life took some getting used to. Every once in a while, though, the nagging voice in her head warned not to get too comfortable—people like Heather didn't change that quickly. When it spoke, she pushed the negative thoughts away. Easier to accomplish as time went by.

Colby slid into the chair across from her and sipped his coffee. His green eyes scanned her face, making her squirm a little. He swallowed the drink, then grimaced.

"Ack, hot."

She giggled, wasn't able to help it; his presence made her nervous. An awkward silence descended. He ran a hand through his hair in his odd back-to-front way as Julie fiddled with the sugar packets.

"It hasn't even been seven minutes yet," she said.

"Huh? I'm not following."

"After seven minutes of conversation, there's a natural pause."

God that sounded stupid. Her hand went to the napkin in her lap and started plucking at it while she waited to be ridiculed.

"Okay, I think I get it," he said. "Let's see how long we can talk *without* a pause."

She relaxed, and they fell into the patter of meaningless chitchat and harmless teasing. An hour rolled by.

"You're different than I thought," Colby said.

"Now that's a bit of a backhanded compliment."

"No, that's not what I meant. I mean I thought you were quiet and shy and didn't like to talk."

A worm of discomfort writhed in her stomach. She wanted the conversation to remain lighthearted, not become serious, so she didn't answer. He took the hint.

"Are you going to the Winter Formal?" he said.

The worm morphed into anticipation. *Is he going to ask me?*

"Of course, it'll be my first one," she said.

"I'm not going." The worm rolled over and died. "They're nothing special, and you wouldn't be missing much if you skipped it. I'd ask you to come watch a movie with me, but I'm going to see my mom in Portland."

"Oh. Well, have fun." What else could she say?

A rap on the window startled her. When she turned, she saw her mom standing there, pointing at her watch.

"I have to go. Thanks for inviting me. I had fun."

"I did, too. We should do this again sometime."

Thinking about spending more time with Colby, she put on her coat and made her way to the door.

"Think about skipping the dance, okay?" she heard Colby say.

She turned to him, "I'll consider it but doubt I'll change my mind. See you tomorrow."

* * *

A cold December full moon looked down on Julie as her high-heels clicked against the frozen pavement of the school parking lot. She shivered when the wind plucked the hem of her dress and flared the material, forcing her to hold the skirt down. The *faux*-pearl necklace Heather loaned her bounced against her collarbone in time with her quick footsteps. Never had the light pouring from the lower windows of the school appeared so inviting.

Once inside, she put her coat in her locker, then followed the muted sounds of "Macarena" coming from the gym. Her stomach fluttered, and she broke out in a light sweat. It coated her skin with a thin film, and she prayed it wouldn't make her itch. The open doors to the gym yawned in front of her

She hesitated.

Heather and the others were waiting inside, but she wanted a moment to savor the anticipation of her first dance before going in. A pair of chaperones exited the gym, glanced at her, and moved on. She was ready. Taking a deep breath, she walked into a room transformed.

Glittering paper snowflakes hung from the ceiling and sprawled across the walls. In the low light, they shone and sparkled, while the silver garland wound around the chair- and table-legs shimmered. The thrones for the Snowflake King and Queen—everyone knew Heather and Tyler were going to win—sat on a dais against the far wall. On either side of the makeshift stage stood giant speakers, and to the left a sound system had been set up on a folding table. Heather and the group were talking with the scrawny senior in charge of the music.

The song faded from the "Macarena" to "That Girl," and the driving reggae beat flowed around her. It lent her confidence, something she'd never experienced but liked. Shoulders back, chin lifted, she flowed around the dancers. Some stopped dancing and, eyes gleaming in amusement, spoke to each other, or nudged their partners. Julie took it as acceptance and stood taller. Heather saw her and waved, a sideways smile playing across her face. She picked up a mic from the table. It dangled loosely from her hand as she walked to meet Julie.

"Nice dress," Julie said. "I like blue on you."

"Nice pearls. They look better on me," Heather said.

In an unexpected move, Heather ripped the necklace off Julie's neck. Stunned, Julie watched the beads bounce on the hard floor.

"Aww, look what you made me do." Heather turned and nodded at the D.J. The music stopped. Heather flicked a switch on the microphone. "Oh hey, everyone, can you believe it, Ghoulie Julie actually came."

At hearing her nickname, Julie started to back away but the kids drew closer to hem her in. Her heart raced and hands shook uncontrollably. She scanned the gym for a chaperone. None appeared.

"What, did she think we really wanted to be friends with her?" Heather's snide voice bounced off the walls.

Giggles and jeers rolled through the crowd.

Trisha sidled up and spoke into the mic. "I mean, like, how gullible can someone be?"

Mandy shook her head and walked away. Julie turned and tried to push her way through the crush of teens. They pushed her back. All around, she saw faces pulled into leers, lips twisted into mocking smiles, and fingers pointed.

All that's missing is a bucket of pig's blood to dump on my head.

"Stop it," she said. "Let me leave."

"Oooh, does little Ghoulie Julie want to go home to her mommy?" Heather said. "Did you know Ghoulie Julie used to have nightmares and would sleep with her mom until she was eleven?"

The muscles in Julie's body tensed as she realized every secret she'd shared with Heather and her entourage was about to be made public. *How could I have been so stupid? Why did I trust them?* On the heels of the thought, the voice of reason said, *I told you so.*

"Don't forget, she wet the bed until she was four," Trisha said.

The crowd broke into rampant gales of laughter. Again, Julie tried to force her way through the throng, and again, they held her back. She changed tactics and tried to grab the mic from Heather. Tyler pulled her away and held her in place. As Heather and Trisha spilled the unsavory aspects of Julie's life, she squirmed trying to free herself from his grasp.

"But enough about her past," Heather said. "It seems our favorite little leper has a crush on Colby. Too bad he's not here."

"Why did the music stop?" Mr. Dean said from the gym doors. "What's going on?"

Relief almost made her sag to the floor as her knees threatened to give out. Tyler dropped her arms and stepped away.

Instead of bolting, she said to Heather, "Why?"

"Because you disgust me. And because I can."

This time the crowd parted for her, and as she ran the tears started. They drew her mascara in their wake, dripped from her chin to leave grey blotches on her bodice. She passed Mr. Dean, barely seeing his concerned expression. He tried to stop her, but she dodged his hand.

"Julie, stop," he said. "Let's talk this out."

She didn't stop, didn't want to talk anything out. Racing down the hall, she held back the sobs that built up in her chest and made her breathing ragged. *Stupid me, stupid me, stupid me,* repeated over in her mind. Julie punctuated each instance of *stupid* with a fist to her thigh. Into the night she went, not noticing the frosty air as it touched her exposed skin, snuck through the thin material of the dress. Unconsciously, she headed toward the one place where she had always found sanctuary: the cliff.

By the time she reached it, her fingertips were numb and her teeth chattered, but she still didn't acknowledge the cold. The wind had died, and the motionless air amplified the sounds of waves breaking on rock. Riding high, the full moon lit the clearing with silver light. Against the black backdrop of the sea, a man and child engaged in a wordless scuffle. She came to a standstill.

The man had the child by the arm and was trying to drag him toward the forest, but the boy struggled to pull free. By the light of the moon, she recognized the man as Colby's father, Mr. Jackson, and the boy as Tommy, one of the twins she sometimes babysat.

Her stomach sank as she seized the truth.

The barely scabbed wound on her heart from the loss of Clare ripped open, and sorrow wound around the anguish from the events at the dance.

Shaking from more than the cold, she stepped forward and said, "Leave him alone."

Mr. Jackson looked her way but didn't release Tommy. Behind her branches cracked and snapped as if something large had barreled its way through.

"It's not what you think," he said. "I'm just trying to get him back home."

Would people ever stop lying to me?

Julie channeled the pain and hurt inflicted on her tonight, thought of poor Clare, and charged Mr. Jackson. Surprise crossed his face, but he didn't move out of her way. Together, they tumbled into a heap on the ground while Tommy spun away, Mr. Jackson's hold broken.

"Stop it, Julie," he said as he tried to get the upper hand. "You're misinterpreting the situation."

"Stop lying to me!"

They rolled closer to the edge. Julie scratched, punched, and kicked at him while he tried to fend her off.

"What did you do with Clare?"

He stiffened for a split second. "I don't want to do this to you. Forgive me."

Mr. Jackson flipped her on her back, straddled her chest, and pinned her wrists down. Small rocks dug into her shoulder blades and wet grass dampened her dress. She heard Tommy's receding footsteps, then the crashing in the forest grew louder. Mr. Jackson looked toward it. His jaw dropped and his grip slackened.

Julie jerked her wrists free, then bucked him off her torso. Still staring at the forest, he wobbled and fought to stand upright, but a huge, hunchbacked body tackled him. The momentum carried them over the edge. He screamed. It grunted. And in the space between Mr. Jackson's shrieks, a single word—*Ulie*—floated up.

Julie went away into a part of her mind she hadn't visited since childhood, blocked everything out, and endured.

The next thing she remembered bright lights circled her, a dog barked, and too many people asked her questions. Blinking, she tried to comprehend what was happening, what they were saying. Her brain wouldn't process anything but the cold. Teeth chattering hard enough to rattle her skull, she rubbed her arms with blue-tipped fingers. Someone flashed a penlight in her face.

"Give this girl a coat," a man said.

Another man draped a heavy coat, warm with body heat and smelling of cologne, over her shoulders. She hugged it to her but the shaking continued.

"What is your name?" the man with the penlight said.

She stared blankly. Again the penlight, this time directed into her eyes.

"Danielle, I need you over here," he said. "I don't know how long the young lady's been out in this cold without a jacket. Let's assume she's in an early stage of hypothermia. Get Brian to help you take her to the ambulance. She may have seen what happened, so watch for signs of acute stress reaction."

A blink, and Julie heard the wail of the ambulance siren. Glare from bright lights stung her eyes and drove nails into her head. An oxygen mask, heavier than she thought it would be, lay against her face. Another blink, and the light softened. Voices to her left spoke in the low, slippery tones of a conspiracy—*for observation, she'll be released tomorrow*. From behind the curtain on her right, came intermittent beeps. She took a breath—*beep*—let it out—*beep*—and let the pattern of breaths and beeps carry her into sleep where she didn't have to think about kidnappers and missing children, and Clare, and Ulie.

The following days passed with questions, answers, and discovery. First, the barrage: How did Mr. Jackson end up at the bottom of the cliff? What did you see? Most of which she answered with *I don't know*; that seemed safer, mentally and emotionally.

Second, the discovery in Mr. Jackson's tool shed of a backpack belonging to one of the missing girls. For one anxious day, Julie and her mom stood outside the perimeter of police tape and watched the men dig. They clung to each other, dreading, yet half-hoping one of the shovels would unearth Clare so they could let her go. The ground yielded nothing except the old bones of a deer. Despite the lack of bodies, the town judged Mr. Jackson guilty, based on the backpack, and Colby went to live with his mother in Portland. Rumor said Colby had broken mentally and begun raving about seeing a monster with glowing eyes in the tool shed.

Christmas came and went. The calendar flipped to a new year, and school began again. Julie wanted to remain buried under blankets in bed with her books, but, since she'd missed the last two weeks before Christmas break, her mom thought it time for her to return.

As Julie walked into the school, the general noise faded into silence. Kids turned to watch her—some whispered, some stared, and some outright glared at her. Shoulders hunched forward, head down; she ignored them and went to her locker. Heather and her entourage waited there. Julie wasn't surprised but wondered where Mandy was.

"Look who dared to show up today, after what she did to Colby and his father," Heather said.

Julie stared at the ground and scratched at a patch of sores on her forearm. After the incident on the cliff, her condition had flared up like it hadn't since childhood.

"Because you said Mr. Jackson took those kids, Colby got all fucked up and is in some hospital," Tyler said.

"I saw him trying to take Tommy," she said, her voice so low she barely heard it.

"You ugly little liar. Mr. Jackson would never hurt anyone," Heather said. Her fingers pinched the lean muscle of Julie's bicep. "I'll bet you pushed him to get back at Colby."

Julie freed her arm and walked away. Angry, demeaning catcalls chased her down the hallway. Exhausted, mentally and spiritually, Julie just put one foot in front of the other. She couldn't do this anymore, couldn't take their shit. *Fuck it.* For the third time in the school year, Julie walked out the door.

Once home, Julie acted on autopilot. She gathered clothing, a few books, the babysitting money she'd squirreled away, and toiletries into an old canvas duffle of her dad's. It smelled of woodchips and grease, and, as she slung it over her shoulder, it made her feel closer to him. A smidge of guilt at the thought of deserting her mom rose and quickly receded. Her mom would be better off without Julie. Besides, since Clare went missing, it wasn't like she noticed, or cared for, Julie anymore. When she locked the front door, the deadbolt engaged with a snick that sounded like finality.

An hour later, she sat on a Greyhound bus bound for Seattle and watched the trees and houses flick by. Superimposed over the scenery, her reflection traveled with her, a silent ghost. When she exited the bus in Seattle, it followed.

Everywhere she looked, people rushed and cars started and stopped as lights changed from green to red and back again. The heavy scent of exhaust clung to the damp air. Buildings towered above her. Definitely different from the small city she'd just left. It intimidated her, made her feel small. *I should go back.* She gave a little snort. *Back to what? The torment?* No, she wasn't willing to return, but her impulsiveness had left her unprepared. She would need to find a place to stay, food, and a job and she didn't know where to begin. Her stomach rumbled. She'd eat first, then plan her next move. And, who knows, maybe she'd meet someone who could help her.

Night arrived too soon. In a corner booth of an all-night donut shop, Julie hunched over a cup of coffee, trying to make herself as small as possible. The place smelled of confections, coffee, piss, and disinfectant. Cracked orange vinyl covered the benches and chairs scattered around scarred Formica tables.

She'd already been there over an hour, witnessed a homeless man urinate in the corner opposite, and watched hookers—at least that's what she assumed they were—warm up before heading out again. Her search for somewhere to stay had turned up empty. None of the low-rent places the waitress from the diner this afternoon directed her to would rent to her if she didn't have a job or an income. And the places hiring help wouldn't take her on without a fixed address. Her babysitting money wouldn't last long at this pace. Maybe she should just go back.

"Hey, gorgeous, why the long face?" a man said as he slid into the seat across from her.

Julie eyed the man. Nothing about him, from the tidy shirt and jeans, neat hair, and wide, non-threatening smile made alarm bells in her head jangle. He looked like a university student, and he had called her gorgeous—no one had ever told her that before.

She sat up straighter and said, "No reason." Despite his friendliness, she wasn't about to tell him she had nowhere to go.

"I don't believe you. Hmmm, let's see." He studied her. "I think you're sad because you have no place to sleep."

"How did you know?" *Why did I just ask him that? Now he knows.*

"The duffle bag gave you away. And if you lived near here, you definitely wouldn't be sitting in this shit hole. It's dangerous at night."

"Oh."

"I'm Richard, but everyone calls me Richie."

He extended his hand for her to shake. His large one enveloped her petite one, and, as they shook, he held her gaze, lingering a little too long for comfort.

"Julie," she said then pulled her hand back.

"Julie," he said, as if tasting the flavor of her name. "Pretty name for a pretty girl."

Her cheeks warmed, and she stared into the bottom of the coffee cup.

"I have a proposition for you," he said. "I know a girl who needs a roommate. She works for me. Would you be interested?"

Hell, yeah. But she tried not to let him see her excitement as she wondered what type of job the girl did. She might be new to the city but she wasn't completely stupid.

"She's not a hooker, is she?"

Richie laughed, then said, "No, she works in my nightclub. Well, my uncle's club, but I run it for him." He paused and studied her again. "We need another girl and you'd fit right in. How old are you?"

Not able to lie well, Julie said, "Seventeen."

"Too bad," he said and got up to leave.

Panic at losing a place, and a possible job, made her jump up. In her haste, she knocked her mug over. It clattered on the table and spun once before stopping. She cringed and expected everyone to stare, but they were too involved in their lives to notice. Richie was almost to the door.

"Wait," she said. She bounced on her heels and fidgeted with the coat zipper. "Do you think it'd be any trouble if I just met the girl? Maybe we can work something out."

Richie flashed another friendly grin, then said, "Sure, I guess. If she likes you, I suppose we can arrange something."

A smile on her face, she grabbed her bag, and, full of gratitude, rushed over to him.

"You're even prettier when you smile."

He put a hand on her lower back to guide her into the rainy night.

The nightclub turned out to be a strip joint, and the girl, Becca Jade, a stripper. Becca pitied Julie and took her in. Richie's "arrangement" included a fake ID saying Julie was twenty-one. Once the ink was dry on the ID, he put her to work bussing tables.

Chapter 5

1997

At the age of eighteen, Ghoulie Julie took to the stage for the first time as *Destiny Starr*.

The brass pole gleamed under the stage lights that cast the men beyond the first row of tables into darkness. She took a deep breath to center herself and calm her pounding heart. The experienced girls watched from the wings. Her stomach churned, and the music started. Every dance step, timed beat, and pole maneuver deserted her. A tense smile on her face, she attempted to find the rhythm. Smooth hip slides turned into awkward bumps. She stumbled on her stilettos, fell into the pole, then clutched it while trying to maintain an air of sexiness she didn't feel. A boo rose from the crowd. Face flushed, she ran off the stage.

Becca followed her to the dressing room and patted Julie's back while she cried. When the jag ended, Becca went to her purse and pulled out a little baggie. She brought it over.

"Try this, sugar," she said. "It'll help."

Julie scrutinized the baggie as Becca dangled it by a corner. White powder, so unassuming and innocent in appearance, filled the bottom half of the bag, but Julie found it repelling. She leaned away from Becca and the coke and attempted to tell Becca *no thanks* but the door to the room crashed open. Richie stormed in.

"What the hell, Julie?" He grabbed her arm and shook it hard. Julie cowered. "I take you in, get you a place, convince my uncle to hire you, and this is how you repay me?" He squeezed until his fingers dug into bone. "You want me to toss your ass on the street? See how you like hooking?"

"Gear down, big rig," Becca said. "We're gonna powder her nose then she'll be set." To Julie she said, "Come on now, sugar, let's get you ready."

Julie watched uneasily as Becca poured a little of the cocaine onto the vanity, then used the edge of a credit card to cut it into lines. She wanted to tell Becca to stop, but Richie's presence cowed her. Every once in a while, he grunted and shook his head as if debating whether keeping Julie was worth it. When Becca finished the prep, she rolled up a dollar bill and held it out to Julie. *Damned if I do and damned if I don't.* She took the bill.

"Okay, show me how to do this," Julie said.

By the time Julie's turn came around again, she didn't need to take a deep breath. Her nerves hummed and jumped, and when the driving beat of her music began, she didn't falter. She closed her eyes and let the music consume her. Hips thrust, clothing slid to the stage floor, hands slid over her breasts, squeezing and toying with her nipples. At one point, she opened her eyes, saw the dollar bills littering the stage, and looked into the crowd. The hunger she saw on the men's faces, in their eyes, filled her with power. They desired her, Ghoulie Julie. She was *wanted.* And they couldn't have her. Smiling, she ran a hand down her side, over her belly then ripped off her G-string as the song ended and the lights went off.

The years fell away in a flurry of white powder and intoxicating power. To stand on the stage, taste the anticipation of the marks, and know she controlled them was more addictive than the coke. The unfulfilled desires of the men empowered her, changed her from the meek little girl into the sleek, confident headline dancer. *Hey Ma, look at me! I've become a dancer just like you always wanted.*

Then there was Richie, always him, for after the second dance of the first night he recognized her abilities and decided she would be his.

Chapter
6

2006

At the age of twenty-seven, a pregnant Julie, aka Destiny Starr, stood on the cliff behind her childhood home for the first time since the incident with Mr. Jackson. She didn't think back to that time, though. Another matter occupied her mind.

The sun's rays hit the calm ocean and sparkled like mirror shards. A gull soared silently overhead as the waves lapped the rocks. Not even a breeze rustled the leaves. She wanted to yell to break the silence. Instead, she swallowed her inner turmoil and rested one shaking hand on the slight baby bump. In the other hand, she held a letter. Her nerves jangled and twitched, and her brain screamed *one little line wouldn't hurt, it'd smooth you out*. She chewed the inside of her cheek in hopes the pain would override the need and read the message again:

> Dear Julie,
>
> If you're reading this, you know the cancer beat me (a cliché but I couldn't think of another way to put it). You're probably mad I didn't try to contact you sooner but when you ran away, I fell apart. You were the last important thing in my life. I've kept track of you for years, took me a while to find you at first, and I'm so sorry how your life turned out. I blame myself. I wish I'd been a better mother to you after Clare was taken. But since you can't unring the bell, as my mom used to say, I want to try to make it up to you by proposing this:

> I've set aside money for you to get help, go to rehab, if not for me than for the baby (Yes, I know you're pregnant), and the house, the studio, and all my assets are yours to do with as you see fit. If you want to turn your back on my proposal, even though I'm gone, I'll understand. After the way I treated you, you don't owe me anything. All I ask is you take some time to think about it. Once you've decided, contact my lawyer at the number at the bottom of the page, and let him know. Whatever you decide, I'll always watch over you.
>
> Love,
> Mom

Julie crumpled the letter, intending to hurl it over the cliff, but a small flutter in her abdomen stilled her angry hand. The cause of the little quiver had killed any chance of her remaining a headlining dancer, where the real money was. Even if she weren't pregnant, the drugs were aging her fast, too fast. And Richie had grown careless with where, and how hard, he hit her, making it difficult to cover the bruises with makeup.

What did she have to lose by accepting her mom's proposal? Nothing. What did she have to gain? A new life, no more running.

Chapter
7

2008

At the age of twenty-nine, Julie snapped. Ever since moving back to Cressidia with little Natalie Jade, Julie had ignored the veiled stares and whispered comments. Didn't let them bother her, knew she was stronger than their curiosity and malice. Until one day in the grocery store, she ran into Heather, Trisha, and Monika.

Irritable, Julie turned her cart down an aisle. Her head ached with lack of sleep—an eighteen month old with the flu, not fun—and the squeaky wheel didn't help matters. Nor did the thought of returning to a house reeking of sour milk vomit. And let's not forget the pile of sheets and all of Natty and Julie's pajamas needing to be washed.

Mrs. Potts had kindly taken Natty off Julie's hands so she could at least get some grocery shopping done. Not that this was turning out to be much of a break. Already, she'd almost snarked at a pair of her mom's old friends who'd, when they saw her, clucked and shook their heads, as if they knew everything. Julie turned down another aisle.

Heather, Monika, and Trisha stood there, grocery carts to one side, chatting. Occasionally, Julie had seen one or another of them in town, but always from a distance and never together. Heather rested a hand on her slim hip while Trisha flicked her brown hair—not a trace of grey, probably a dye job—from an unlined forehead. Julie smoothed the front of her stained t-shirt and tried not to feel the left-over baby bulge. The trio stopped talking, glanced her way, then started whispering.

She heard snippets of the conversation. *Ghoulie Julie…Winter Formal…Mr. Jackson…stripper…Destiny Starr…drugs.* Anger, embarrassment, and fear—all the seventeen-year-old Julie's emotions—rose and fell in a jumble while she pretended to study the cereal and tried not to let them get to her. But she was exhausted, and, at the word *whore*, she lost it.

"Say that to my face, Heather," Julie said, stepping forward.

Heather, spite in her narrowed eyes, said, "You're nothing but a whore."

Three quick strides brought Julie to Heather and fist to nose. Cartilage snapped with a pop—*Fuck! That felt good*—then bright red blood flowed. Heather cupped her nose. Monika pulled out her phone. Trisha went to Heather. Julie just smiled.

"I dare you to say it again," Julie said.

"Heather, don't," Trisha said.

But Heather pushed Trisha away, lifted her chin, and, despite her obvious pain, said, "You'll always be a whore."

"Thank you," Julie said then her fist eclipsed Heather's eye.

Chapter 8

2010

At the age of thirty-two, Julie spoke to Richie for the last time.

Natty lay curled against her on the little cot in the dance studio's office. One chubby, eczema riddled hand curled under her chin and the other tucked under the pillow. Rubbing Natty's back, Julie waited for her to drop off into a morning nap. She stared at a crack in the ceiling and thought how Natty had changed her life. How if she'd aborted Natty like Richie wanted, she'd probably be a hardcore, washed-up dancer stripping in a dive for drug money. The studio definitely wouldn't be hers, either.

When Julie first inherited the place, she intended to put it up for sale but decided against it. Partly because in some small way, holding onto it kept her mom's memory alive and partly because she needed something to occupy herself after rehab. Initially, she had a rough time battling the temptation to slide back into drugs while trying to balance the studio with taking care of an infant. Eventually, she managed to acquire a talented group of instructors, ones she trusted and whose personalities meshed. Once the studio returned to the lucrative state her mom had known, she had hoped to go back to school and get the degree in psychology she always wanted, but then came the craze of women wanting to learn to pole dance. Who would have thought pole dancing would become so popular among bored housewives?

Natty sighed and turned onto her back, her little eyelids fluttering with a dream. Julie kissed her forehead, then gently rolled off the cot and stood. Instead of taking advantage of the quiet to pay bills, she changed into bike shorts and a crop top and headed for her classroom.

The doors to the four classrooms, two per side, sat open and the darkness within the large spaces seemed to shift. Julie shivered as she passed them. Goosebumps rippled down her back. Her ears strained to hear past the ominous silence while she half expected something to reach out of one of the darkened classrooms to grab her. The normally calming scents of sweat, shoe leather, and hairspray did nothing to quell her growing trepidation. The atmosphere carried the same type of charge as the strip club right before a fight broke out.

Don't be stupid, Jules, there's no one here but you and Natty.

Mad at herself for getting the heebie-jeebies, she slammed the light switch, and the soft glow of the overhead track lighting dispelled the shadows. Jaw clenched and a frown on her face, she strode to the stereo, selected In This Moment—a heavy-rock group with a sultry female lead—and cranked it up. Soon the opening beats surged from the speakers. In the mirror, she watched herself perform one of her former dance routines, one she didn't teach her students. She tapped into the full strength of the old power, something she rarely did, since doing so left her with a bad taste in her mouth and a case of the guilts.

The song ended and rolled into the next one and the next. Sweat glistened on her skin; and long, defined dancer's muscles rippled along her arms and legs as she hung upside down, spread-eagle, from the pole. Platinum blond cornrows, tied together with an elastic, dangled toward the floor. She slowly tipped her legs back then flipped over and landed on her feet to slide into a measured hip grind. Loud and calculated clapping from the doorway caused her to jump.

"*Brava,*" Richie said over the music. "You can come work for me anytime, babe."

"Fuck you," she said as she used the remote to turn down the music. "How'd you get in?"

"The front door. How else?"

Julie glanced at the wall clock. It was after eleven and her receptionist, Linda, would have arrived by now.

She glared at Richie as she said, "What are you doing here?"

"Can't a father come and visit his daughter? How is little Natalie Jade doing?"

"I smell bullshit. You only show up when you need something from me, which is only about once a year, and you already put in an appearance this year."

"A person can change."

Julie fought not to snort, "You? Change? Yeah, right. Oh, wait a minute, it appears you have. The bald look suits you. Finally, you look like the smarmy perv you really are. Con any young girls lately?"

Richie laughed and sauntered into the room, giving her the once over. Never knowing what to expect with him—a slap or kindness—Julie felt an adrenaline surge but stood her ground.

"I like this spitfire side of you. It's hot."

"Shove it. Why are you really here?" Her hands shook. She rested them on her hips to mask their quaking.

Richie smiled at her just like he had when she was seventeen. Long ago, she'd found it charming; now it only disgusted her.

"I came to offer you a job."

"Nope, sorry, not interested. I fought to get out, get clean, stay clean, and start a new better life for Natty. Not going to throw that away." He raised his eyebrows at her mention of staying drug-free.

"Just hear me out." He didn't wait for her to reply. "I've built quite a large cliental with my private porn business. I have a few premium clients, and one of them saw that old sex tape you and Becca Jade did. Remember that?" Julie wished she didn't. "Good times, babe. Anyway, for some reason he's infatuated and has requested you and some girl-on-girl action with a *very* specific kink. What he'll pay will probably put Natalie Jade through college."

Anger at his audacity turned the tips of her ears bright red and brought a prickle of tears.

"Forget it, Richie. I'm not whoring myself out."

A knowing smirk tugged at his lips as he reached into an inside jacket pocket. She wanted to slap it off his face. Out came a small baggy filled with coke. A tremor shuddered through her. His smirk morphed into a smile.

"Let's relax a little, have some fun. Maybe you'll change your mind." He dangled the bag like a dare, a taunt.

Another little quiver shook her as she recalled the euphoria … the *power* … the drug gave her. Four years, and the craving for the sweet, sweet sensation of flying high, the world at her feet, men on their knees before her, hadn't diminished. Disgusted at herself, she shoved Richie's arm away.

Taking the time to enunciate each word so he'd get it, she said, "Get the fuck out now."

"Daddy?" Natty said from the doorway. Sweat-soaked bangs clung to her forehead and sleep crusted her eyes.

Shit.

"There's my little princess," Richie said. He palmed the baggie and slid it back into his pocket. "Wow, you're looking more like your mom every day."

Inwardly, Julie scoffed. *Like you'd know how she changes day to day, shithead.* Then her heart broke a little when Natty launched herself at him. Richie knelt and caught her in a stiff hug.

"I miss you," she said into his shoulder. And Julie's heart broke a bit more.

"I miss you, too, Princess."

"Then why don't you come visit more?"

Go on, tell her why. Julie crossed her arms. She wondered what excuse he'd give.

"I'd love to but Daddy works a lot," he said. He disentangled himself from her arms, stood, and patted her head. "Mommy and Daddy have to talk. You go wait for me in Mommy's office."

Natty grinned up at him. "Okay. You can see the picture I colored all by myself." She scampered off.

"We have nothing to talk about," Julie said. "You should go say goodbye to your daughter and leave."

He ignored her suggestion. "If my client can't have you, he's going to walk away. That won't be good for me. Come on, Jules, just do this one thing for me and I'll go away forever."

"Go fuck yourself."

Julie stormed from the classroom and shut herself in the office. A minute later, he pounded on the door.

"Think of the money. Think of Natalie Jade's future." When she didn't answer, he changed tactics. "Do it for me." And when she still didn't reply, he switched it up again. "You're a whore and always will be. Nothing can change that, might as well accept it and come get this thing done."

She knew he was wrong, but the words stung. She leaned her forehead on the door to keep from ripping it open and screaming at him.

Finally, he said, "Fine then, be a bitch." He slammed a hand against the door and left.

Not moving, she silently cursed him to Hell.

The office seemed to shrink, to encase her like a coffin. Her lungs squeezed out short shallow breaths and her heart drummed in her ears. The image of the tempting white powder Richie had dangled in front of her made things worse. She needed to get out of here. She tensed at a small sob from the cot. *Natty. Damn him.* She turned. Natty sat holding the picture she wanted to show her dad, tears streamed down eczema-stained cheeks.

"Why'd Daddy yell and go away? Didn't he want to see my coloring?"

Julie went to her and wrapped her in a tight embrace.

"Oh, sweetie, no. I made Daddy leave. He wasn't being nice."

"Will he come back when he's nicer?"

Julie rubbed Natty's back while she debated whether to tell her the truth or a lie. She settled on the diplomatic middle ground.

"I don't know. Let's say we go get some ice-cream."

"With sprinkles?"

Ah, the resilience of kids.

"Yup."

Natty wiped her nose on Julie's shirt, then skipped to the door. As Julie went to change into her street clothes she couldn't help but think, *it's you and me against the world, kiddo.*

Chapter 9

2013

At the age of thirty-four, Julie lost what little she had left. And found what she had lost.

The pungent aroma of garlic bread from their spaghetti dinner lingered in the kitchen. From the little radio atop the fridge, Oasis's "Wonderwall" rose to its finale. Julie stood at the sink washing the supper pots while a sullen Natty—*seven already, makes me feel old*—dried and put them away. This moody Natty bothered Julie, made her wonder if something had happened at school. Afraid to ask yet more afraid of the answer, she instead squeezed a dollop of dish soap onto her fingers, mixed it around, then dipped her fingertips into the water.

"Watch this," Julie said.

She made a circle with her index finger and thumb and blew. A bubble formed. It broke loose from her hand to float in the air. They watched it bob and weave and when it popped in a shower of soap, Natty giggled.

"Do it again," Natty said.

Julie did. Natty clapped her hands.

"Let me try."

Picking up the soap bottle, Julie said, "The trick is to balance the soap and water. Too much soap and it'll be too thick for a bubble. Too much water…."

"It will be too thin."

Julie smiled. How could she chastise Natty for interrupting with the correct answer?

"Smart girl. And if you blow too hard?"

"It'll pop before it'll float."

"How did you get so wise?"

Natty rolled her eyes. "Come on, Mom, just gimme some soap."

"Huh, wise but needing to remember her manners."

"Plleeease."

Julie upended the bottle over Natty's hand, but a newscaster on the radio caught her attention: "…Andrea Dickens, Celeste's mother, said Celeste wasn't in her bed this morning when she went to wake her up. Anyone with information on the seven-year-old Celeste's whereabouts is asked to contact…."

The blood draining from Julie's face made her cheeks feel cold. She put a hand to her chest as if to keep her hammering heart on the inside, while a panic attack attempted to sweep her into its embrace. Happened every time she heard a child had gone missing no matter where in the country the report came from.

Natty smooshed the detergent between her fingers, "I forgot to tell you. I found a giant lady in the forest. She couldn't open her eyes so I did it for her." Obvious pride shone in her voice. "She ran away. It made me sad."

Natty's words didn't fully register, but Julie nodded as if she'd heard them. She gripped the counter's edge to keep from sliding to the floor. *Breathe, Jules, pull it together.* Natty ceased talking and stared.

Noticing concern in her daughter's wide-eyed expression, Julie put on a smile. "Let's get this bubble show on the road."

The remainder of the evening sped by, yet simultaneously crawled. Once Natty had bathed and Julie had read her a story, Julie paced the house. *What if it's beginning again? Don't be an idiot, Mr. Jackson is dead. But what if he wasn't the kidnapper?* She didn't want to contemplate the possibility; she'd seen him trying to abduct Tommy. *But what if…?* The question turned around and around in her brain. She began another lap of the house.

In each room she went through, she saw her childhood overlaid with the present. Her mom's chaotically organized mess jarred with Julie's fastidiousness. Gone from the living room were the second-hand furnishings. Instead, more contemporary pieces offered her and Natty comfort. In the kitchen, no more 1970s

Formica countertops or dark, wood-paneled cupboards; in their place were light grey countertops complimented by blond wood cupboards. She'd kept the maple dining table, a family heirloom. The office had been converted into a spare room since she preferred to work at a desk in the living room. Natty's room—Julie's old one—reflected her personality; and Clare's, Julie left empty. Despite that, she still saw Clare whenever she glanced in.

Clare with her curls bouncing as she skipped after Julie, pestering her with questions, bugging her, begging for Julie's attention. If only Julie hadn't been so wrapped up in her own problems, she might have given more time to Clare. Maybe Clare wouldn't have felt the need to climb out her window after Mr. Jackson. *What if it wasn't him?* Or maybe Clare had simply been looking for a father figure and it had nothing to do with Julie. As it was, she could only look back with unanswered questions and watch the ghosts of the past chase her from room to room.

* * *

Startled awake, Julie lay in the dark and wondered what woke her. Thinking it was nothing, she tucked one hand under the pillow and closed her eyes.

"Mom!"

Julie jumped out of bed. The sheets tangled around her ankles, almost tripping her. She cursed while disentangling the sheet and trying not to topple over.

"Mom!"

"Coming!"

Feet free, she dashed to Natty's room and flicked on the light.

"What's wrong? A nightmare?" Excitement danced in Natty's eyes as she shook her head. "What then?"

"Someone tapped on my window."

"Are you sure?" Julie's voice cracked, and she hoped Natty didn't hear the fear.

"Uh-huh. They had glowing eyes. Like Superman's laser vision."

Julie leaned a hand against the wall to keep from sagging to the floor with relief. *A dream, that's all. No one's coming to kidnap Natty.* Yet a deeply buried memory from childhood stirred. It attempted to show her a seven-year-old Julie—*Ghoulie Julie*—in pee soaked pajamas. She shuddered and shunted the image deeper into her subconscious.

Natty—oblivious to her mom's reaction—babbled on. "Maybe it was Superman looking for me. Maybe he wants me to help him. Maybe Wonder Woman was here, too. That'd be cool."

She went to Natty, kissed her forehead, and tucked her in before saying, "They probably need your help but the only way you can do that is when you're dreaming. So let's go back to sleep and see what they need."

"Yeah, I can be The Dreamer, that way no one can hurt me 'cause no one can hurt you in your dreams," Natty said, her eyelids growing droopy. "I'll rock."

As Natty fell asleep, Julie sat on the edge of the bed and watched the window with trepidation. Half-expecting to see glowing red eyes peering in, she ran a hand through Natty's hair, her fingertips riding over the all too familiar hills and valleys of scabs. Once Natty's breathing smoothed out, Julie got up to turn out the light but stopped. She took a good look around the room, and, like every time, a pang of sorrow stabbed her soul.

Superhero posters, especially of Wonder Woman, covered the walls, and figurines stood guard along the shelf of books and comics. Julie knew Natty was too young for some comics and kept a tight rein on which ones they bought. However, who was she to deny Natty of her superheroes? Sometimes you needed a superhero or two to help keep the bad guys away and, after all, at the age of seven she'd had She-Ra.

Julie turned off the light.

On her way back to the bedroom, it struck her how much stronger and light-hearted Natty was compared to herself at that age. With all her heart, she wished Natty would take the initiative to talk to her about what was going on. If there even was anything amiss. Rationally, she knew it was wrong of her to put it all on Natty. After all, Julie was supposed to be the adult. She hoped

Natty wasn't talking because she wasn't going through even half of what she had because of the eczema. The superheroes told otherwise.

* * *

Winter rained its way into sunny spring. Celeste still hadn't been located but the cops were working on some solid leads, or so they told the media. In the meantime, another little girl disappeared, and rumors started spreading. With each passing day, the feeling of history repeating itself grew.

"Alright, I'm outta here to go pick up Natty," Julie said to her receptionist. "Have the girls call my cell if they need anything."

Julie pulled open the door and walked out into the day. A brilliant flash of sunshine dazzled off a car bumper, momentarily blinding her. She collided with a figure standing in front of the studio. Before she could fall, a hand cupped her elbow, steadying her. Feet firmly planted again, she shielded her eyes and prepared to let loose a rant but stopped. The man looking down at her reminded her a little of Egon from the old Ghostbusters movie, but beyond that seemed familiar. From the expression on his face—squinted eyes and pursed lips—he recognized her as well.

"Ghoulie Julie?" The question sounded more like an accusation than a query, and it rankled her. Then he ran a hand through his hair, back to front.

Colby. Oh, this is just great. She shouldn't be surprised since she'd heard he was back in town. Not that she'd kept track of him, but sometimes information seemed to come her way. Word at the café was his mom had recently passed away and left him his dad's old house. He'd come to fix it up, then put it on the market. She couldn't imagine he would want to keep the place and didn't blame him.

"Haven't been called that for a long time. I have to run," she said. "Have to go pick up my daughter."

"My dad didn't do it, Ghoulie Julie."

The repetition of her old nickname and his obvious rejection of the truth, even after all this time, caused the muscle in her jaw to tick. She stepped back, although she hadn't avoided confrontations since high school. Feeling like the awkward teen of yesterday, and hating it, she took another step and prepared to pivot away from him.

"It wasn't him. I was with him on the night Clare went missing, but no one believed me," he said.

"You have no right to say her name. Your father tore our family apart when he took her."

"I'm trying to tell you he didn't do it."

Julie fought against the rising anger and lost.

"Oh, get off the denial train and accept it was him." Colby cringed, then thrust his chin forward. She thrust hers out also. "I saw him try to take Tommy. Remember?"

"Bullshit. Tommy used to sneak out all the time, and Dad would go fetch him for Mrs. Rooney when Mr. Rooney worked the graveyard shift. But no one believed me."

At the anguish in his voice, she softened. "The backpack the cops found in his shed told a different story. I'm sorry—it was your dad."

Julie spun on her heel and walked away.

"The monster put it there. The hairy one with red eyes," Colby said so quietly she almost missed it.

For a brief, seemingly eternal, moment her mind's eye saw Mr. Jackson fall in slow motion over the edge of the cliff. Her ears heard his scream and another voice calling, *Ulie*. She turned back.

"What monster?"

"Nothing. It's started again even though my dad is gone. Doesn't that tell you something?"

Crossing her arms, she stared at him. He met her gaze. In it, she saw he really believed what he'd said.

"You really are convinced that some monster stole those kids, and now it's come back." Two names reverberated from the past—*Yani, Ulie*—bringing unexpected terror at the recognition *she* might be the one in denial. She buried it under sarcasm. "Oh, Colby, that's so sad."

Colby growled. "I don't even know why I bothered seeking you out. You fucking ruined my life, and it sounds like you'll continue to." He stalked off, denying her the chance of rebuttal.

A strangled cry struggled to break free, and she stifled it with the back of her hand. Her lips felt cold against it. *He's crazy. That's all there is to it.* After reiterating it to herself a couple more times, she squared her shoulders and went to retrieve Natty.

***

Spring morphed into an unusually cool summer. No additional little girls went missing—*thank God*—lulling the residents of Cressidia into thinking there would be no more abductions.

The slap of sneakers on pavement startled the robin, sending it winging into the air only to vanish into the fog. Too early in the morning for traffic, Julie ran along the centerline, her steps falling in rhythm with the heavy-metal music pouring from her earbuds. Sweat slid onto her lip. She tongued it off and tasted the sharp salt of her sweat mingled with the saltiness of the ocean. Sections of the road appeared and disappeared at the whim of the fog, and in one such unveiling Julie glimpsed a muted glimmer.

She slowed and pulled the earbuds out. Curious, she trotted to the object on the ground: a pink sneaker with a silver charm attached to the laces, looking forlorn and abandoned on the cracked asphalt. The shoe disturbed her and an immediate sound of gravel grinding underfoot unnerved her. Wary, she glanced over her shoulder.

The fog parted enough for her to catch a glimpse of a brownish hide bounding into the woods. A deer. She laughed with the release of nervous tension, only to have the sound swallowed by the mist. Dense silence followed, pressed down on her and felt like loneliness. The urge to return to Natty overrode the mystery of the discarded shoe and the obsessive compulsion to run which drove her out of the house each morning. She slipped the earbuds into place. The music lent a false sense of company as she ran home with the feeling something other than the deer watched her go.

Julie tugged the earbuds out and let herself in through the side door. She pulled off her runners and made her way to the kitchen. The time between the calm of having a still-slumbering daughter and the craziness of getting her ready for school when she awoke was Julie's favorite part of the day. It gave her a moment to putter around and think undisturbed.

She flicked on the radio and started a pot of coffee. The maker gurgled and hissed in competition with the music. Feeling lazy, she pulled out the cereal reserved for weekends as the morning news began. Time to wake Natty.

"Natty, honey, time to get those lazy bones out of bed. It's not summer vacation yet." Julie knocked on Natty's door. Silence. "Answer me or I'll come pull the covers off you."

Natty hated that and usually responded with a giggle and a *No, don't.* Julie hesitated.

"Okay, here I come." Julie opened the door. Blankets lay twisted in a heap at the foot of the bed and one pillow rested on the floor.

"Natty?" Julie said, hoping her daughter had hidden in the closet, waiting to jump out and scare her. "Not funny, sweetie, come out and get ready for school."

A curtain billowed in, then out. Her heart stopped—*no, not Natty*—then rolled and resumed beating with painful thumps. *I didn't check the bathroom.*

"Natalie Jade!" She crossed the hall.

Julie flung open the bathroom door. Empty. Turning back to Natty's room, Julie saw the curtain flutter again. For a moment it confused her, then she sprinted to the window and pushed the curtain aside. With bile stinging the back of her throat, she stuck her head out and looked down. A smattering of wildflowers lay strewn on the ground, a large footprint mashing a buttercup into the soft earth. Two sets of prints led across the grass and to the forest. Julie threw up.

* * *

The days and nights ran together in a confusing twist of *déjà vu* and stark reality. Only there wasn't anyone to hold her on the couch, pat her back, and say it'd be all right, that they would find Natty.

Even having Richie around would have been better than sitting alone, but last year his luck had run out. His illegal activities had caught up with him and he was sitting in some cell in King County Jail. Once again, she dealt with tragedy on her own.

Cops tramped through the house, the backyard, and forest, while the phone rang and the doorbell ding-donged incessantly from the well-intentioned dance moms and dancers. Julie unplugged the phone and considered smashing the doorbell but couldn't find the hammer. Instead, she ignored them, but that didn't stop visitors from leaving casseroles and lasagnas on the stoop. Every morning a new batch cropped up. When the freezer couldn't possibly fit another dish, she took to feeding the men and women searching for Natty. It gave her something to do since she'd been banned from the hunt.

The forest had echoed with the calls for Natty. Twigs had crackled under Julie's feet as she'd followed a pair of men. Their orange hunting vests bright in the cloud dimmed light.

"Poor woman," she'd heard the taller man say. "First her sister, now her daughter."

Tears had built along Julie's lower lid.

"Heard she used to be some crazy-ass druggie stripper in Seattle," the other man had said. She'd slowed. "Heard she almost killed some dude for touching her." She had clenched her jaw. *Then he'd heard wrong.* "Maybe she's always been *off*, if you know what I mean?"

"I'm not following you."

Julie had stopped.

"You know. Maybe she had something to do with her sister and daughter's disappearances."

The past had roared into the present forcing her to relive the first day of senior year when she'd crouched on a toilet and heard almost those exact words come from Heather.

All around Julie everything had gone white until the only color left was the man with the accusation.

On the balls of her feet as to make no noise, Julie had rushed the man and tackled him to the ground. His partner had pulled her off him before she had the chance to do anything more than slap his cheek. They'd dragged her kicking and screaming back.

Julie felt her muscles tense and twitch with anger all over again. It was so unfair the organizers banned her when it should have been the asshole. She was Natty's mother, not him.

After wiping tears of frustration from her cheeks, she poured coffee into a thermos to take outside.

* * *

Heather and the others, including Danny and Tyler this time, caught Julie bringing a fresh thermos of coffee to the volunteers. Other than trading icy stares on the few occasions they'd run into one another in town, this was a first.

"What do you want?" Julie said when they reached her.

"We need to talk," Heather said. "I've tried calling…."

Julie continued pouring coffee into paper cups, "There's nothing to talk about, so why don't you do me a favor and fuck off."

"See, I told you this was a bad idea, hon," Tyler said. "Don't waste your time."

"Shut up, Tyler," Heather said. The tone of her words suggested that she told him this often. "Look, Julie, we're all hurting here. Celeste is my niece and Leanne is Danny's. Strange, huh, all three missing girls being connected to us."

In her grief, Julie hadn't noticed the coincidence. Unlikely she would have on her own, it wasn't like she kept in touch with these people. And certainly didn't know enough about them to know who their nieces and daughters were. While it intrigued her, she found it difficult to muster compassion for Heather and Danny.

Too many bad memories. But maybe the heartache of losing a loved one had changed them, so she set aside the past and gave them a chance.

"Fine. What do you want from me?" she said.

Heather smiled, a tired ghost of her former manipulative dazzler. "We want to go to the media and the social networking sites. We'll tell our story, how we were friends in high school and now our nieces and daughter are missing. You can even mention Clare's story. Maybe we can garner national attention and support. We might be asked onto talk shows. We'll be famous."

The brief idea that they might have changed vanished; Heather's motives were purely selfish. What sane person would put fame over finding the girls? Julie clenched the fist not holding the thermos and took a step away, while telling herself not to throw coffee in Heather's face.

"First, we were *never* friends in high school," Julie said. Heather's eyes widened in surprise. "Oh, don't look so shocked, you know how you treated me. Second, using Natty, Celeste, and Alice's disappearances to gain fame is fucked up. Third, Clare is not connected to this. So, like I said before, why don't you all fuck off."

"I guess that means you won't help?"

"You guessed right."

"Not even to be one of us?"

"What the hell? Are we still in high school? I don't need your acceptance or your friendship. I don't need anyone."

"Please reconsider," Monika said. "It will look better if all three of you are involved."

In lieu of a reply, she glared at each one in turn. Tyler grabbed Heather's shoulders and pointed her toward the driveway.

"Time to leave," he said. Heather dug in her heels. "You're not going to get your way this time, so let it go." She huffed but let him lead her away.

After the group departed, Julie noticed the silence. The volunteers stood watching her.

"Show's over," she said, then plunked the thermos on the volunteers' table and stormed into the house.

Julie paced around the kitchen. *Damn, Heather.* She grabbed dirty mug and rinsed it under the tap. *I should have walked away before she opened her mouth.* Heather's words circled and echoed. Julie heaved the mug against the wall and slid onto the floor. Watching the pieces of ceramic spin to a stop, she wept.

Natty, where are you?

* * *

Ten days into the search, Julie woke from the light doze passing for sleep with the feeling that some new thing was amiss. She checked the clock—mid-morning. Three hours of fitful sleep was a record. Fighting the urge to curl up, she pulled herself off the bed to see if the volunteers needed anything.

For once, the sun made an appearance to warm the air. It brought bees out to buzz around the potted roses and tickled her skin with its heat. Soaking in the rays for a moment, the darkness in her mind dissipated. They'd find Natty and the other two alive, scared, but alive. She moved into the backyard.

The young cop they'd had manning the volunteer table was now breaking it down. Unobserved, she watched him fight with one of the legs, a bead of sweat tracing its way down his thick neck. A satchel lay on the ground, and she saw a clipboard—the one with the volunteer list—peeking out. The forest was quiet. No echoing calls for Natty. A boulder settled into her gut and her optimism vanished.

"Where is everyone?" she said.

He startled then looked up at her. "I'm sorry, ma'am, we've called off the search. One of the officers found evidence to suggest that your daughter's been taken out of town."

The rock in her stomach sank to her feet. *No, that's not right. I can feel her here.*

"She couldn't be. She's somewhere in the forest, I know it," Julie said.

"I'm sorry, ma'am, but the evidence suggests otherwise."

"Do you always start your sentences with *I'm sorry*?" The anger that the search had been ended made her snappish. He didn't answer, but then his previous words hit her. "Hey, wait. What evidence?"

"I'm…I apologize but I'm not allowed to disclose the information. One of the lead detectives will be in contact soon."

"Sure you can. I won't tell anyone." Shaking his head, he finished folding up the table. "Come on, this is my daughter we're talking about. I have a right to know."

"I'm sorry, but I have my orders."

He picked up the satchel then for the first time seemed to really notice her. His gaze crawled from her head to toes and back up. She knew the look. Subtly she dropped her shoulders down and back, a move from the stripping days that accentuated her chest, and let him ogle. There were many ways to get information out of a man.

"Like what you see, officer?" she said in a soft voice. Opening her eyes wide, she sucked in her bottom lip then slowly released it.

"Actually, I was wondering…. When was the last time you looked after yourself?" She frowned. "I'm sorry, but you look like you haven't changed or showered in a week."

Her ego deflated, and not just because she *hadn't* showered in a week. In spite of everything, she still didn't care for rejection. He tossed the satchel over his shoulder before picking up the table, and the action niggled a memory she couldn't quite catch.

"For what it's worth, ma'am, I hope they find your daughter safe," he said. "Have a good day." He turned to walk away.

"Not likely."

She watched him round the corner and stride out of sight. The emptiness of the backyard, with its trampled grass and a lone paper coffee cup, brought her reeling to reality.

No one was searching for her daughter anymore. She'd have to find Natty on her own.

But a surge of despair crippled her. First her dad, next Clare, then her mom, and finally Natty, all gone. What was the point of putting one foot in front of the other and fighting anymore? Too tired of being strong, of battling life and losing those she loved, Julie chose to do what she did best when faced with difficult situations.

She ran away.

* * *

Cocaine sparking along nerves and well-worn jeans hugging her ass, Julie climbed out of the taxi and strutted into the Coyote Bar and Grill. She thought it a stupid name for a non-country bar out on the West Coast, but, for this summer at least, it was the happening spot for those in their thirties.

On the stage against the far wall, the band went through a sound check as the lead guitarist tuned his Gretsch White Falcon. Conversations hummed around the room, low for now, but as the night wore on, they'd grow louder and rowdier. A miasma of floral, woody, and musky perfume and cologne scented the air but didn't quite hide the sour smell of stale beer. Spying an empty stool by the bar, she sauntered over. The old tingle of being watched and appreciated danced up her spine. She smiled as she slid onto the stool. The men seated on either side checked her out. *Funny what a shower and a tight pair of jeans can do for a girl.*

Unconsciously wiggling her jaw from side to side, she flicked the cornrows over her shoulder, trying to catch the bartender's eye. When he came over, she ordered a shot of tequila and a bottle of Corona. The golden liquor warmed her belly and amped up her already lit senses. She swiveled around and leaned back into the bar to observe the crowd as the band started up with their rendition of "American Woman." Her interest in crowd-watching vanished into the pulse of the music. Time to dance.

She plunked her purse on the bar and said, "Keep an eye on this for me will you, gentlemen."

The scraggly-bearded older man on the right winked and tipped his beer bottle at her. She took it as a *yes* and hit the empty dance floor. By the time the opening chords of "Roxy Roller" surged from the speakers, a few other dancers had joined her. She lifted her arms and shimmied her hips, earning more than a couple glares from some of the ladies present and admiring stares from the men and even a few women. Losing herself to the song, she turned the hip shimmy into a sultry circle and deliberately worked the room. If it bothered anyone, why should she care? Knowing any one of the men, or women, single or attached, would take her home if asked filled the hollowness inside.

Songs began and ended, and on she danced, until the edginess of an imminent comedown crept over her. Leaving the dance floor, she retrieved her purse, made sure the seat would be saved, then wound through the throng to the bathroom. A little bump and she'd be golden.

Inside a bathroom smelling of piss, vomit, and hairspray, Julie joined the short line of women waiting for a stall. Her foot tapped a restless beat on the tile as she switched her purse from one shoulder to the other and back again. *Hurry the fuck up would you.* After what seemed like eons, the next available stall was hers.

She slid the lock and hovered over the toilet seat as she peed and rummaged around her satchel for the baggie. *Damn it, where is it?* Concentrating on the task, she didn't hear the door beside her bang closed nor the low feminine giggles and male chuckle. Bladder taken care of, she flushed while debating whether to dump her purse onto the floor. Her fingertips brushed the corner of the baggie ending the quandary.

Nose powdered, she swiped the excess off the top of the toilet-paper container and rubbed it into her gums. A moan echoed from the next stall.

"That feels good, Trisha," said a voice Julie knew.

A pause, then Trisha shushed Tyler. Flying high and feeling good, Julie swallowed the threatening laughter but couldn't contain a small snort. Julie tiptoed out of the stall, washed her hands, and, as she exited the bathroom, nearly bowled Heather over. Not about to let Heather ruin her high, she tried to keep walking but Heather blocked the way.

"Watch where you're going," Heather said then realized to whom she spoke. "Funny seeing you here. I would have guessed you'd be too concerned about Natty to be out, or have they found her?"

Julie balled her hand into a fist, forced it to relax, then said, "And why aren't you at home working on getting famous off the missing girls?"

"You're getting tiresome, Ghoulie Julie. Why don't you just go away?"

Heather flapped her hand in a shooing gesture. Julie stayed put and watched Heather's features twist in a snarl at being disobeyed, then she smirked.

She cocked her head at Julie and said, "I saw you dance earlier. You should go back to stripping. The coke-head-whore look really suits you."

The desire to deck Heather tempted Julie but she decided to jab her where it really counted. "If you're looking for Tyler, you might want to check the woman's can. Trisha's there, too."

Heather's mask crumpled and the pain written on her face surprised Julie.

"I know," Heather said. A wan smile flickered across her lips. "Now go away."

Taking no pleasure in Heather's pain, although she had every right to, Julie walked away. Halfway back to her stool, Heather began yelling at Trisha loudly enough to be heard over the pounding rhythm of the band. The crowd moved against Julie as they surged to see what the fight was about, but she managed to push through. Sliding into her seat, she ordered a couple more shots of tequila.

The rest of the night flew by in a kaleidoscopic blur of tequila, dancing, and trips to the washroom to powder her nose. By the time the bartender announced last call, Julie felt as smooth as a pane of glass; only the thought of returning to an empty house caused a small jag. She'd fix that. Julie checked out the men who'd sat beside her all night and settled on the one to the left. Thinning blonde hair, brown eyes, stocky, not really her type but he'd do in a pinch. Besides, he hadn't pounded back the beer and shots like the other one.

"Hey, sugar," she said as she put a hand on blondie's shoulder. "Care to give a lady a ride home?"

Shortly after introductions were made, Stewart held open the door of a Camaro older than her and she poured herself in. They took off with a chirp of tires while AC/DC's "Shook Me All Night Long" provided an excuse not to talk.

The headlights flashed across her little Honda in the driveway. She got out of Stewart's car and stumbled up the front walk.

"Steady, girl. Let me help." He put his arm around her waist.

"I'm fine."

Julie twisted away, but the combination of coke and tequila threw her off balance. She landed on her ass next to Natty's plastic picnic table, almost knocking it over. Stewart caught it before it fell.

"You have kids?"

"A little girl, Natalie Jade."

At the mention of Natty, all the fun went out of the night…or maybe it was the coke wearing off. Whichever, Julie crawled up the front steps and used the doorknob to pull herself up. She felt around for her key while Stewart appeared to mull something over.

"Isn't she one of the missing girls?"

"That would be her." She found the keys and wondered if she'd snorted all the coke.

While she attempted to coordinate key to lock, Stewart snuggled up behind her, took the key, and unlocked the door.

With the anticipation of a bump consuming her, she forgot about Stewart and instinctively made her way through the dark living room to turn on a lamp. Stewart stepped inside, shut the door, and watched her upend her purse onto the coffee table. She sifted through random bits of paper, lip gloss, and receipts, panicking. *Where is it?*

"What are you looking for?"

Ignoring him, Julie moved an old tissue and found the baggie stuck to her credit card. A dusting of power coated the inside and a smidge filled one corner but it might be enough. She hoped.

"Sorry, babe, not enough left to share."

He reached inside his coat, then set a vial on the coffee table.

"You were holding out on me." She gave him one of those crooked grins that sent marks into fits.

She moved to take the vial but hesitated.

"Go ahead. This one's on me."

She prepared the coke, then handed him a rolled-up bill.

He waved it away. "I don't snort my product."

"Whatever," she said and bolted down the rabbit hole.

* * *

Nights and days wove around one another until they became a single high. Julie handed the care of the studio over to her instructors with only a vague mention of when she might return. If the detective called to talk to her about the evidence that Natty had been taken out of town, she didn't remember. Weight dropped off her already slender frame, giving her a haunted look. And Stu was always there to supply her when she came up empty and keep the bed warm when she needed it. The thought of finding Natty faded into nothingness. Her present sank down to greet her past.

A ray of sunshine glared through the window and stabbed her in the eyes. Groaning, she attempted to unglue her tongue from the roof of a very dry mouth and roll over at the same time. Coordination wasn't her friend, and she toppled onto the floor. The scratchy blanket slid down with her and, eyes remaining shut, she rested her head on it. *When did my bed get so small?* Julie opened her eyes a crack. A coffee table leg stared back at her. *Didn't even make it to bed. Jules, hon, you've got to pull your shit together.* But the pounding in her head wouldn't allow her to think straight. A *Good Morning* bump would fix that, then she'd get herself put together.

Using the coffee table as a crutch, she heaved her body upright and scooted onto the couch. Beer cans and white smears littered the tabletop, and all the little baggies were empty. *Damn it. Where's Stu?*

"Stu, hey, Stu." She hated the sound of need in her voice, yet didn't care either. "You still here?"

The toilet flushed, the bathroom door creaked, and he came into the living room. He wore one of his work suits, one she called his restaurateur-chic look, but when she bothered to think about it, he never mentioned which restaurant he owned. Must not do very well if he had to deal coke on the side.

"I'm just on my way out," he said.

She blinked at him as she struggled to accept that it was already afternoon, not morning like she'd thought.

"Could you leave me with a fix?" When he didn't reply right away, panic nibbled in her. "Please. I'm hurting here."

He rubbed his jaw and looked past her at the photos on the wall.

"I have a novel idea. No more coke for you until you pay me. It's been two weeks so I figure it's time."

"Just float me one more and I'll get you the money by tonight." Her mind already figuring out which bank account could take the hit.

Stu shifted his gaze to her and sent her a cocky sneer reminiscent of Richie when she said something he didn't like. She knew what was coming next and scooted to the other end of the couch, then he altered the sneer into a smile. It knocked her off guard.

"I have a better idea. A business proposition, if you will. I know you used to strip and you teach pole-dancing to hard-up housewives, so why don't you work off your balance by dancing for me?"

While the tension ran out of her shoulders, Julie regarded him as if he'd come from another planet. "Really? That's it? So do you want me to dance for you now or when you get back tonight?"

"You're so cute, Jules. No, I meant at my club."

She must have given him a dumbstruck look because he laughed. "You don't remember me telling you I own the Frisky Business."

Aww, fuck, now everything makes sense. Sorta.

"I'm too old. You need someone young with a firm body."

Stu chuckled. "Nothing wrong with your body. Anyway, I don't run a high class place. Bikers and truckers mostly. You'll do just fine."

His words cut through her headache and, not knowing whether she was insulted, ashamed, or just in dire need for a pick-me-up, allowed the anger, that good old standby, to rise. She jumped off the couch, her shin hitting the coffee table and sending beer cans clattering to the rug.

Standing on her tiptoes she looked Stu in the eye and said, "Fuck you."

He laughed in her face.

"You're in no position to fuck anyone. You're nothing but my whore now."

She swiped at his jaw, but he grabbed her wrist and squeezed. Bones ground together, making her knees sag and tears spring to her eyes. A purple vein in his temple bulged.

"Don't ever try to hit me again."

Flinging her wrist away, he delivered a stinging backhand to her cheek, knocking her to the ground. Tears pouring and nose clogging with mucus, she drew her knees up and hugged them.

"Get the hell out!" she said between hitched breaths.

"There's still a matter of payment."

"Fuck your *business proposition*. I'll get you cash."

Stu smirked, then waved a hand in disgust, and made for the door. Before leaving, he turned. "Since you have more interest in coke than your daughter, you'd have made a wonderful addition to my stable. I hope you change your mind."

The door slammed behind him. He and his coke left.

Heart pounding, in a sweat-induced panic, she crawled toward the door to reach it before he drove off. Halfway there, she stopped. *What am I doing? What have I become?* Julie didn't like the answers to those questions. They told her she'd become everything she hated—a coke whore—everything she'd worked so hard to get away from to give Natalie Jade a chance. Shame burned through her, made her feel tiny. *Natty, I'm so sorry. Mom will make it up to you.* She just didn't know how yet.

Swiping the tears from her cheeks, she vowed never to run again when life took a rough turn. It was beyond time to stop. If not for herself, then for Natty. *But it would be so much easier with coke,* the needy part of her whined. She ground her teeth and tried to will the little voice away but the emotional rollercoaster of withdrawal held tight. From her long-ago stint in rehab, she knew if she didn't find something to occupy herself, she'd give in and head out in search of a fix. Then like a diver coming up from the depths of the sea, she saw—really saw—the condition of the living room.

Beer cans lay in a jumbled mess on the coffee table and floor, blankets on the couch, food-crusted dishes—Stu's since she barely ate under the thrall of the monkey—and dirty clothing scattered willy-nilly. *Perfect.* She set to cleaning and, when the coke monster bubbled up and screamed across her nerves, she gritted her teeth and repeated Natty's name like a misplaced echo. The distraction worked until she ran out of things to clean, including herself.

Julie tossed the wet towel on top of the washing machine. The smell of soap and feel of scrubbed skin and fresh clothing felt good, but they did nothing for the restlessness consuming her. Absently scratching at the joint between forearm and bicep, she paced through the house. Her nails broke the skin and blood stained her fingertips. She didn't notice. Natty's name fell from her lips in a whisper and, as the need to smooth her jagged mind raged, became a yell, then a scream. She stopped pacing, stopped screaming.

Why am I here ranting like a madwoman when I could be out looking for Natty? Such a simple question with a simple answer. She felt stupid, then guilty, because she should have been searching for Natty in the first place, instead of partying. Julie pulled on her runners.

For the first time in a long time, Julie entered the forest of her childhood. Her feet instinctively found the old deer path. Twigs cracked underfoot bringing her back to days when the woods were her playground and imagination ruled…not this madman, this beast, who had kidnapped her daughter.

Twilight touched the woods, spread its gloaming fingers around the trees and brush, muting the browns and greens. Birds sang as they flew to their roosts to settle in for the night. Like the ticking of a slowly dying watch, the world around her wound down.

"Natalie Jade! Natty!" she yelled.

Part of her knew too many days had passed for Natty to still be within shouting distance. Part of her hoped Natty had gotten away and was trying to find her way back, waiting to hear her mom's voice to bring her home.

"It's mommy. You can come out now!"

Around and around she wandered and yelled while, with each circuit, the cocaine monster released its grip. Her feet started to pick up the pace until the trees sped by and her heaving gasps kept her from shouting. The brush thinned and the clearing atop the cliff loomed. Julie skidded to a stop. Waves crashed against the rocks, a hollow boom echoing and matching the emptiness inside her. She crumpled.

Nightmare images clawed to the surface. A cast-aside Glo-Worm. Running through a cold winter night while humiliation burned in her chest and tears froze on her cheeks. Mr. Jackson and Tommy, yelling, then Mr. Jackson falling. *Ulie.* Then Colby on the sidewalk. Her head snapped up. She knew who had the girls. *That son of a bitch.*

* * *

Julie stomped on the gas. The car shot around a curve, tires chirping as they slid on the dry pavement. Knuckles white from gripping the wheel and forearms shaking with tension, she blew through a stop sign and raced on up the hill toward Colby's childhood home. She had worked out the timeline and the reasons why Colby would kidnap the girls, especially Natty, and the logic made sense to her.

The house came into view. A shiver skated along her muscles as she remembered the last time she'd been to the house. When the police were digging up the ground to search for bodies and she and her mom stood on the outskirts and held each other. Clare and Mr. Jackson. Natty and Colby. Life had a weird way of circling back sometimes.

She cranked the steering wheel, missed the driveway, and ended up on the lawn. Tires ripped out chunks of grass and left muddy valleys in their wake. Before the car stopped, she slammed it into *park*. The vehicle shuddered and the engine stalled. Julie threw open the door, charged up the steps leading to the porch, then fought not to fall into the pit where the porch should have been. Arms wheeling and toes curled over the edge of the top stair, she wrestled against gravity. *What if Natty was already dead and buried in the dirt under the ripped-up boards?*

Julie forced her weight into her heels, leaned back, and stumble-fell down the stairs to land on the grass. After catching herself, she went back up the steps and peered down. A smudge of light from the living room window illuminated the dirt enough for her to see boot prints but no freshly turned earth. Relieved, she gripped the banister to keep from falling again. However, anxiety wormed its way in. *Did he have the girls in the house? Was he hurting them right now?* She turned and jumped from the step. There had to be a back door.

Sprinting around the side of the house, she kicked over a couple of paint cans stacked one on top of the other. They clattered together, the metallic rattle loud in the still night. A dog began to bark with a deep *roop-roop* from the yard next door. She heard a window slam open, then a man yell for Magnum to shut it. She hoped he hadn't seen her. Magnum kept barking.

When she rounded the corner, a stadium-bright floodlight clicked on to cast the yard, and its unassuming shed, in *faux* daylight. Julie leapt up the steps to the back porch. For a second she expected the boards to have been torn up as well, but one foot landed solidly. She opened the screen door and hammered on the inner one. It flew open. The door rebounded from the wall and she stopped it with a hand. She bounced on the balls of her feet while debating whether to call out—but then he'd know she was here—or go inside and surprise him.

He could charge her with trespassing but she didn't care. She went inside.

The silence of an empty house greeted her, yet a dim light found its way into the laundry room where she stood. She followed the glow.

It led her to the kitchen. Cupboards, their doors removed, displayed plates, cups, and bowls on the left and the meager staples of one not planning to stay long on the right. A little girl's pink shoe lay on the counter. Her heart plummeted. Next to the shoe was a tool belt, screwdrivers and a hammer stuck in the loops. Brown splotches marred the bright metal.

She bent to inspect the tools, the space inside her rib cage feeling as if someone scooped out her innards and replaced them with lead. Julie scratched one of the marks with a fingernail, then let out a shaky breath. Rust. If there had been someone with her, she would have hugged them. But there wasn't anyone accompanying her, no one to warn her if Colby was sneaking up behind, knife in hand, maniacal leer twisting his lips.

The absence of sound suddenly seemed sinister. Julie took a step back and rubbed the goosebumps that a sudden violent shiver raised on her arms. Out of the corner of her eye, she caught a fluttery movement in the room beyond the kitchen. Muscles tense and heart thudding in her ears, she turned to see the sheet tacked above an open window billow in the breeze. Her body slumped, as if every bone had been replaced with gelatin. Strained laughter slipped from her throat, the sound of someone on the verge of panic. It snapped her back to reality. *What the hell am I doing playing vigilante? Stupid, Jules, very stupid.* The back door never seemed so far away.

She thought of calling the cops—soothing thoughts—while she tiptoed back through the short hallway. The sound of a door slipping shut followed by a shriek, a thump, and the noise of frantic scratching ripped the quiet. Julie stumbled, then her legs locked up. The clawing continued, and she found the will to move.

"Natty!" Forgetting her fear she headed deeper into the house.

Down another short hallway a staircase led upwards. She stood at the bottom, wondering whether he'd hold the girls upstairs or in a cellar.

The screech came again. Definitely upstairs. Julie took them two at a time. Panting, she paused at the top and saw yet another hallway.

A drop cloth covered the floor, with paint cans stacked in a small pyramid, the brushes lined up beside it. The earthy, chemical scent of paint almost overpowered the whiff of decay. Julie hoped to God it was dead rat and not dead Natty or any of the other girls. *Old, closed up houses attract rats. Right?* Insane laughter hovered, ready to tumble out.

Three closed doors on the left and two on the right. The middle door on the left rattled as something hit it. Not thinking or caring about her safety, she flung it open and prepared to wrap Natty in a tight embrace. Instead, a white cat streaked out of the dark room.

A fucking cat. Giggles bubbled to the surface. *A goddamn fucking cat.* They rolled out of her, loose and shrill, and when they crested a questioning *meow* sounded. Her throat closed. She choked and whipped toward the stupid animal, ready to give it shit, but the anger died. It wasn't the cat's fault.

The cat *meowed* again then wound its way over, a deep purr in its throat. It head butted her knee, and Julie bent to scratch it behind the ears, eliciting more happy rumbles, but then it hissed and sprinted away. *Fickle thing.* Forcing herself to accept Natty wasn't upstairs, she started to close the door—didn't want poor pussy to be trapped again—but the room wasn't as dark as she'd first thought. A faint blue glow emanated from within, as did the scent of something dead. Torn between curiosity and the need to leave, she hesitated. Then, convinced it would only take a second, she went inside.

The light came from a computer screen that'd been left on so she picked her way over to it hoping it might give her a clue as to where Colby held the girls. Partway across the room, she brushed against a form. It spun and twisted, then struck her. Her eyes adjusted to the dim light and she screamed.

Colby swung in lazy circles. Under the blue light, the mottling on his face took on a black cast and the cloudy corneas of his bulging eyes seemed azure. Pinned to his chest, a note printed in childish block letters: "They're my friends now." Her scream morphed into an almost soundless squeak as the implication slammed into her. *Suicide. Fuck no, Colby. Who'll tell me where Natty is now?*

The room went black.

Before her imagination reanimated Colby, the whir of the computer fan kicking in, overlapped the rope's creak, and the monitor flashed back on. The lighting flickered and settled to a steady glow. From her vantage point she couldn't see what was playing on the screen, but as she struggled to figure out how to get to the computer without touching the body, it went dark again. A pause, then light. Something—a video perhaps—was cycling but how? Colby must have been dead for days, and any computer she ever used would gone into sleep mode after a certain length of inactivity. This one should have, too.

A mindless fog took command of her feet and guided them to the computer. At first, only an empty backyard flickered on the screen, then a shadow appeared. It grew and elongated until its owner crept into view. Julie figured the person—*it was a person, nothing else*—to be at least six-and-a-half feet tall, if not seven, naked, and covered in auburn hair. A pink shoe dangled from one hand. The form darted into the shed, and, when it emerged a minute later, its hands were empty. It paused and, almost like it knew the camera was there, stared into the lens. Glowing red eyes looked out from the screen at Julie.

Yani.

For so long she had convinced herself that Yani had been an imaginary playmate, something a lonely little girl conjured up for company. To admit that Yani existed meant she had to accept that her friend had broken a promise and abandoned her, rejected her. And had to acknowledge that Yani was the one responsible for Natty's disappearance, for Clare's, and all the others. Deep inside, she knew Colby hadn't committed suicide. He was Yani's victim and, against her earlier convictions, so was his dad.

The initial shock wore off as Julie regarded Yani's image cycling across the screen. When Yani appeared again, Julie paused the video. Despite the proof—the child's shoe—she had trouble believing Yani had abducted anyone. It didn't jive with her now resurgent memories of her friend.

But she also remembered Yani, eyes aglow, ordering her to get into the basket. Julie had seen the hint of another side to Yani, one that created fear. The recollection of being afraid of her friend cemented in Julie's heart that Yani wasn't what she appeared. She was quite capable of kidnapping.

Downstairs, the back door slammed shut. The fog broke. *Yani. She was here all along.*

Julie sprinted from the room leaving Colby's body to swing in her wake. *Where's Natty, you bitch.*

She bolted down the stairs, leapt the last treads, landed perfectly, then raced to the back door she'd left open. It was closed, just as she'd expected. She twisted the knob and dashed into the bright light. Where the glare dissipated, a pair of glowing red eyes looked back at her.

"Yani, wait!"

The eyes blinked and Yani ran away.

Julie started after her but stopped. It was futile to chase Yani through the forest at night, especially when she knew where Yani was headed.

* * *

Ulie and Yani.

At the age of seven, Ghoulie Julie had found a naked girl whose eyes were sewn shut, then lost her.

At the age of fourteen, Ghoulie Julie had stopped searching for the girl with the cedar basket, then forgotten she existed.

At the age of thirty-four, Julie, no longer Ghoulie Julie, hunted down the girl, now a woman, who had taken her daughter.

Flashlight in hand, Julie tore through the underbrush toward the place she'd first discovered Yani. The sphere of light bounced and bobbed across tree trunks, and branches scraped her arms. They broke the skin and left shallow, stinging lacerations. Blood seeped to the surface and attracted mosquitos. The small clearing—it had seemed much bigger when she was seven—came into view. Julie slowed.

"Yani, it's me, Ulie! I'm here!"

Julie stopped to listen. Tumbling waves, a buzzing mosquito, but no sounds of something crashing toward her. Did she really expect it to be that easy?

Desperation made her beg. "Give me Natty back. Please. I know you have her."

The skin on the back of her neck tightened, and her scalp tingled with the feeling of being watched. Julie turned in a slow circle and scanned the woods.

"I know you're here. I can feel you watching me."

Halfway around the second rotation, she spotted the glint of metal. The belt Julie had left for Yani twenty-seven years ago twisted from a low-hanging branch. A reminder of a time when two shunned little girls found a friend in each other. She yanked it from the tree. The cloth had rotted in spots, the buckle had tarnished in places, and a long auburn hair clung to it. The belt recalled memories of friendship, laughter, and games…replaced by images of the missing girls. She shook off the nostalgia.

"Where are you?" she yelled.

Leaves to the right rustled. *Gotcha.* Julie dove toward the sound. The belt buckle bit into her palm, and twigs dug into her knees as she skidded across the forest floor. *How is it I always wind up on my knees?* She came to a stop, not at Yani's feet as she'd half expected, but at the side of the cedar basket.

She never thought Yani might have left it as a trap. She threw the belt away and plunged into the black maw of the basket.

Instead of hitting a cavern floor, Julie spiraled through a seemingly endless void. She howled when the darkness closed around her and began to squeeze. *What have I done? Mommy's sorry, Natty.* Bones cracked, organs shifted, and Julie screamed under the compressing blackness. Her cheek pounded onto something solid, and the rest of her body followed. The constricting sensation disappeared.

Birdsong filled air sweet with the scent of cherry blossoms, and sunshine warmed her skin. Keeping eyes shut, she rolled onto her back and assessed her body for damage. Toes and fingers wiggled, her innards didn't hurt anymore, all seemed normal. She opened her eyes, expecting to be at the mouth of Yani's cave, but saw a canopy of flower-laden branches above her. Pink petals drifted down like fragrant snowflakes. The breeze twirled the petals and whispered how nice it would be to rest a minute and, perhaps, to sleep. Of their own accord, her eyelids fluttered closed….

An image of Natty brought her awake and to her feet.

Don't sleep now, Jules. If this is the orchard near the cave, you're almost there.

She scratched at her eczema, what might be the best way out of the grove, then stopped. *Wait. What?* Except for random patches here and there when stressed out, she had outgrown the affliction years ago. She looked at her arms and forgot about the itchiness as the scab-encrusted limbs of a child came into view. *What the hell?*

"Oh look, Wife, she's wondering what's going on," a man said.

"Amusing isn't it, Husband?" Wife said.

"Very much so."

Julie searched for the source of the voices while recalling the magic Yani had used on her so she'd be able to understand this world's language. *I can still follow it after all this time. That's some powerful spell.* Finally, she spied two figures winding their way hand in hand toward her. Their black hair fell like a cape around bodies as naked as they'd been the first time Julie laid eyes on them. The child in her wanted to run away, but the adult saw them for what they were. She almost felt bad for Yani; after all these were her parents and no child deserved the treatment Yani received from them.

When they reached Julie, Wife said, "Oh look, Husband, she'd not afraid of us."

"A wee little thing like that should be, Wife."

"Me afraid of a couple of bullies? I got over that years ago."

They looked from Julie to each other; unspoken words passed between them.

"Maybe we should just leave her to the trees," Husband said.

"Yes, they like little girls."

Yani's father ran a long, slender finger down the bark of one trunk. Julie swore she heard the tree scream and looked closer. The pattern on the bark resembled a girl's face repeated over and over, up and around. Creepy but not scary. Julie turned to the next tree to see if it was the same, and her knees locked. Clare's face wound up the trunk like a demented barber pole. With a shaking hand, Julie stroked the cheek of one of the many Clares. Two thousand tiny blue eyes opened and a thousand tiny mouths screamed. Julie ran.

"Wait! Don't go, wee one!" Wife yelled.

Fuck that.

Grief clogging her throat, Julie didn't stop. The atmosphere tugged at her; a multitude of eyes followed her. Branches rattled in her wake and seemed to whisper she'd be happier if she joined them, they so loved little girls. She ran deeper into the grove. The further in she went, the older the trees became. Brown bark bleached to grey, and cataracts clouded the eyes tracking her passage. Husband and Wife materialized in front of her. Julie bit her lip to keep from screaming. She halted.

"If you want your daughter back, want to save her from joining Clare and the others in the orchard, you must listen to us," Husband said.

"Do you? Will you?" Wife said.

Chest heaving with sobs and her heart double-whamming from the run, Julie nodded.

"Good girl," Husband said.

As one, they turned her around and, a hand on each shoulder, marched her forward.

"Where shall we begin, Husband?"

"Let's start at the beginning, Wife."

"Yes, let's. I love the beginning. You start."

"From the inception of time there was us. The people through the ages call us by different names but we are simply Husband, Wife, and Child. Gods to some, myths to others but benign, good. Only, as Child grew she became naughty evil, and refused to obey, so we banished her to the cave. There she made a cedar basket and started to steal human children, then lied and said she was lonely and wanted someone to play with."

"Those poor Haida peoples. For a time, she only snatched their children."

"So we made her seven again and, as a precaution, we put her to sleep by sewing her eyes shut."

Another tree opened green eyes and watched them pass. It was Celeste. *Poor Heather.*

"If that witch Malika hadn't stumbled into our World, Child would still be sleeping. But Malika felt sorry for Child. So she concocted a means to send her to your world, then cloaked herself from our magic," Wife said.

"She hated us," Husband said.

"At first it didn't matter whether Child was in your world; she was still asleep."

"But then you came along and set her free." Husband's hand gripped harder. "You should not have been able to do that. Your world holds no magic." His hand dug further into muscle, then he relaxed his grip.

"And you should not have been able to travel here, wee one. Human adults cannot pass through."

"That you showed up as seven-years-old must have been Child's doing, but we're digressing. Continue, Wife."

"After you awoke her, we humored Child and, since she stayed seven, watched to see if she'd changed. She hadn't, but Child had learned to deflect our spells so we weren't able to sew her eyes shut again. As you aged, so did she."

"Not until we found her at seventeen, body shattered, and laying outside her cave, were we able to perform the ritual and resew her eyes shut," Husband said. "Then that bitch Malika interfered again and, with your daughter's help, it started all over again. Only this time, Child remained an Adult."

"You're different and we don't understand it. Your daughter as well. You have to end this. We can't."

Something about the tale rang false, but as long as they were leading her to the cave, she'd keep her suspicions to herself. "Fine then. How do I finish it and get my daughter back?"

They came to the edge of the trees. Hints of sunlight rippling off the creek twinkled between the trunks. Yani's parents released her but stepped in front of her before she could bolt for the cave. Wife flicked her fingers at the air, and a shimmery pocket appeared. Husband dipped his fingers into it and withdrew a needle and thread.

"With these." He handed them to Julie.

The needle appeared to be pure silver and the thread simple catgut. Julie assessed its strength. *Okay. Teflon-tough catgut.* She didn't dare test the needle's point.

"When it's time, you'll know what to do," Wife said.

With the cave in sight, Julie asked the one question that gnawed at her.

"Did you banish Yani and sew her eyes shut because she was evil or because she wasn't beautifully perfect, like you?"

Yani's parent's eyes flared red. Julie recoiled and, shifting her weight to ready for flight, contemplated taking her chances in the orchard. Then the quadruple glow flickered out. They laughed.

"Oh, wee one, you entertain us so," Husband said.

"Just sew her eyes shut, and we will make sure you and your child get safely home," Wife said.

"If you fail…." He didn't need to finish the threat. Julie understood.

"And we will know if you fail," Wife said.

There wasn't any walking off into the sunset or fireworks or fanfare; they simply popped out, leaving Julie staring at the creek. Needle and thread in hand, she ran through the ankle-deep grass to Yani's cave.

At the mouth, she resisted the urge to call Natty's name and run pell-mell to the fissure at the back. She tucked the needle and thread into a jeans pocket and crept forward, eyes searching the dark corners for Yani. Deeper inside she went, leaving all but a meager bit of light behind. She reached the fissure, squeezed through, and entered Yani's domain.

The room had changed yet remained oddly the same. The grass pallet now large enough for adult Yani, and the number of wondrous and strange objects had grown. A series of paintings on the walls, however, chilled Julie's heart. They depicted two girls and told Yani's and Ulie's story as seen through Yani's eyes. Julie stretched onto her tiptoes to see it better.

The first showed Yani in the sheet dress, holding hands with Ulie in the clearing. They smiled at each other and played games…until the day on the cliff when the boys threw rocks at Ulie. The next scene depicted Ulie visiting Yani's world for the first time. The one after that showed Yani—mouth drawn in sadness— alone on the cliff. In the next, she again stood on the cliff, anger evident in the slash used for her mouth.

Yani went to the cliff and waited for me?

The following pictures portrayed the kidnappings, then the frightened girls running away and changing into trees. After each segment, Yani had drawn herself crying. But the images barely registered as Julie struggled with the knowledge Yani hadn't deserted her; she'd gone to the cliff to wait. Julie lifted her hand to trace the one of Yani on the cliff, but a muffled sob stopped her, brought her back to why she was here.

"Natty?"

The crying stopped.

"Where are you, honey?"

No answer. Julie scanned the small cavern but initially saw nothing. At second glance, she noticed one of the stone shelves wasn't flush with the wall. She rushed over and—heart fluttering like a sparrow's—peered behind it.

There was a space large enough for one very small person or a child. Natty gazed back at her with wide eyes. Dirt streaked her cheeks and forehead, her bound hands and ankles. Once-blonde hair hung in ratty tangles about a tear-stained face and clung to the filthy bit of rag used as a gag. Natty screamed into the restraint, her nostrils flaring and eyes widening even further. Julie didn't think. She grabbed Natty by the calves and hauled her out.

"Oh, Natty, baby, sweetie, Mommy's here," she said as she untied the gag. "I missed you so much." Julie kissed Natty's cheeks over and over.

Natty bit her.

Julie recoiled as if she'd been shot.

"You're not my mom. You're a stupid kid. I want Yani," Natty said. Julie felt her heart break a little.

"Natty, sweetie, I am Mommy. Yani's magic made me seven again." Julie plucked at the knot binding Natty's hands. *Damn thing's tied tight.* "I've come to take you home."

"I don't believe you. My mom's big and strong, and Yani said she wasn't ever coming to get me." Natty stared at her knees and whispered, "Yani knows magic—that makes her a superhero."

"Then why did she tie you up?"

"To keep me from the evil trees that ate her other friends."

Julie bit her tongue to keep the hurt, angry words from flying out as she sat cross-legged to get at the knot better.

"I love her, and we're going to live here forever, and she'll be my new mom and teach me magic. No one will make fun of me again." The echo Julie heard in Natty's statement cut. "I don't want my real mom to come get me anymore."

"But your real mom misses you so much."

"How do you know? Did she tell you?"

"Because I am your mom, sweetie. I told you that."

"No, you're not."

"Let's see, if I wasn't your mom I wouldn't know you giggle when you fart in the tub."

Natty cracked a smile. "All kids do that."

"Okay then, you like spaghetti but not lasagna and your favorite color is pink."

The binding around Natty's wrists fell away and Julie moved to the ankle bonds.

"You're a good guesser."

Julie wracked her brain for the one thing to convince Natty. And there it was.

"Wonder Woman is waiting on your shelf for you to come home, so is Superman. They need The Dreamer's help."

Natty's muscles tensed. She lifted her head and gazed into Julie's eyes, flicking back and forth between them as she searched for the truth.

"Mommy?" Her face crumpled, and she broke into heartrending sobs. "Yani told me that you hated me and thought I was ugly and were never coming for me." Natty hiccoughed. "Why didn't you come sooner?"

"Yes, why didn't you?" Yani said, her voice guttural, deep, yet unmistakably female.

Julie squeaked as she jumped. *Damn it, I should have been listening for her. Too late now.* She leapt to her feet, a retort dying in her throat when she saw Yani for the first time since they were girls.

At seven feet tall, Yani towered over her. The light cover of auburn hair had grown into a thick pelt from which the nipples of Yani's pendulous breasts peeked out. Her face, however, remained mostly clear, with only a dusting of fine hair from chin to hairline. Maroon eyes flickered between menacing glow and normal. The cedar basket lay by her feet.

"Come on, Ulie. Tell your daughter."

Guilt twisted like a well-honed knife.

"Fuck off, bitch. None of this would have happened if you hadn't started kidnapping girls. Then or now."

Yani's eyes flared red. "No! None of this would have happened if you'd met me when you said you would."

Yani waited for me. Is this my fault? She remembered why she had missed their meeting.

"I had strep throat. I couldn't leave my house, but when I got well, I waited and waited for you to come back for me. I thought you had abandoned me."

"Liar. You were just like my parents and thought I was too ugly for you." Yani narrowed her eyes. "Clare didn't."

"Yeah, and that's why she ran away and ended up as a tormented tree."

Julie hunkered, centering her weight.

"I'll never forgive you for Clare."

Julie pounced. She aimed for the big woman's waist, thinking to bring her down, but Yani side-stepped. Julie missed. The momentum forced Julie into the wall. Bright spots danced at the edges of her vision as she thudded to the ground. She shook her head to clear it, then bounced back onto her feet, ready to attack again. Yani stood—shuddering and grunting—on the other side of the fire pit. *Damn, she moves quick for a big woman.* Julie stared, half terrified and half curious.

Abruptly, Yani's bones cracked like ice. Natty whimpered. Thick auburn hair receded into skin, full breasts shrunk, and Yani contorted. When she rose, it was as seven-year-old Yani.

"Clare might have run from me, but Natty wouldn't. She loves me." Yani settled onto her heels. "She's my friend now."

"No! She's my daughter and I'm taking her home."

As one both girls leapt at each other. They collided above the cold fire, then—arms entangled—rolled across the floor in a ball, each trying to gain the upper hand.

"Mom! Yani! Stop it!" They stopped. Natty had untied her ankles and crouched in the corner. "You're scaring me."

Julie took advantage of the hesitation to spin Yani onto her back then—knees on Yani's wrists, butt on stomach, and hands on shoulders—pinned her down.

"Get off me." Yani bucked.

"Ooooh, I hear fighting, Wife."

"I wonder who's winning?"

Hearing the voices, Yani, Julie, and Natty froze into a curious tableau.

"Grab the cedar basket and hide behind the shelf, sweetie," Julie whispered. Yani's nostrils flared but she didn't move. "That basket is our way home. Quickly and quietly now."

"Can we bring Yani?"

"We'll see. Go on."

Natty didn't need to be told again.

"Yes, take me with you," Yani said. "Don't leave me here." She flicked a glance at the cavern opening.

"Fuck that. If you hadn't kidnapped Natty and Clare and the others, things might have ended different." *Hold up, Jules, for years you thought it was Mr. Jackson. But Yani killed him. Yeah, probably trying to protect you.* She frowned at Yani. "Why did you frame Colby's dad, then Colby. Why did you kill them?"

Yani gazed over Julie's shoulder. "Jealousy. Colby really liked you. I heard him fighting with the others about some dance, and it hurt. He could have you and I couldn't. So I hid the backpack, hoping the cops would arrest him, not his dad. Then Colby came back. You can figure out the rest."

Julie removed a hand from Yani's shoulder and palmed the needle and thread from her pocket.

"It's awfully quiet in there all of a sudden, Husband." The scrape of pebble on rock sounded in the room. "Shall we go see what's happening?"

"Wait, Wife."

The needle pricked Julie's palm, as if reminding her. A drop of blood slid down the side. Yani saw it.

"No, no, no! You're not going to sew my eyes shut. I don't know what my parents promised you, but they lie."

"Now you're the liar."

"Trust me."

"Prove it."

All the tautness left Yani's muscles. "I can't." She fetched a sight so deep Julie felt like it came from her soul. "Don't put me to sleep, Ulie. Please, kill me instead."

Just as Yani's tension had dissipated, Julie's blood drained from her extremities, leaving them pale and cold. *No matter what she's done, I can't kill her.*

"It's still quiet, Husband. Now?"

"Shhh, something's about to happen. I can sense it."

Julie sat back. Instinct told her Yani wouldn't try to get away, yet part of her hoped she would.

"When you didn't come back, I thought you hated me," Julie said. "You were my only friend, the only one who'd play with me. I can't kill you, Yani. But I can't take you with me, either. You'd be treated as a freak, something to be poked and prodded by researchers."

"I can't do this anymore. I can't keep finding friends and losing them, and I can't let my parents put me to sleep a third time." Yani's chest heaved as she fought back a terrible sadness. "I don't want to be ugly anymore."

The question Husband and Wife weren't able to answer tumbled out. "Why me?"

"Because you're the only one who can."

Julie understood. *We're a part of each other. Me, her and her, me. All because we were born different and were shunned for it.*

"Malinka knew this and sent me to you. Later she made sure Natty found me, because she's different like us."

The two girls—each reliving personal pain and the kinship they had found in each other—gazed into one another's eyes.

"Please, Ulie?" Yani's voice was anguished.

Julie made her decision.

"Are you sure?"

"Yes."

Tears pouring from her eyes and snot running from her nose, Julie—Ghoulie Julie—Ulie—picked up a big rock from the fire pit. She so didn't want to do what Yani asked but didn't want Yani to live in torment either. In performing this act of mercy, maybe, just maybe, Julie could be set free as well.

"You're really, really sure, Yani?"

"Really, Ulie. Let me go. Let your past self go."

Yani turned her head, exposing her temple. Julie lifted the stone—large in her child's hands—as high as possible.

"I always thought you were beautiful," Julie said. She brought the rock down, and a double roar shook the cavern.

Despite the howls, Julie heard the stone crush Yani's skull. Yani's eyes changed from maroon to red. *Oh God.* Bile rising in her throat, she brought the rock down again and again until black blood spurted and the glow in Yani's eyes faded to pinpricks.

"No, you are," Yani whispered.

The light in her eyes died, and with it the little rejected girl Julie had once been. Julie cried out, opposing forces pulling her body in a tug-of-war of stretching muscles and cracking bone. It stopped. Sweating and shaking, she let the rock slip from her adult-sized fingers.

Another pair of bellows echoed. Julie glanced toward the fissure, where red light shot with ebony shadows danced at the edge like the water reflecting on a ceiling.

"Mommy, you're big again!"

Julie whipped around. Natty had poked her head around the shelving. When she noticed Yani, her bottom lip quivered.

"Wee one disobeyed," Husband said.

At the sound of his voice, so close, every hair on Julie's body stood up. Her heart threatened to stop.

"Get in the basket, Natty."

"Why is Yani dead?"

Oh crap.

"I don't have time to explain. Just get in the basket. It will take you home."

Natty froze, her gaze fixed behind Julie. Julie turned and saw Husband and Wife entering the room. Gone were the beautiful creatures they had once been. In their place, two versions of Yani—red eyes aglow—pinned Julie with their stare.

"Please go, Natalie Jade. Everything will be all right. I promise."

When it looked like Natty wouldn't listen, Julie scowled at her. Natty went.

"You failed us," Wife said.

"We told you we'd know if you did."

She backed toward Natty's hiding place.

"No, I set Yani free."

"How should we kill them, Wife? Quick or slow?"

Julie didn't wait around to hear the answer. She ducked behind the shelf. Natty had righted the basket and was crawling inside. When her daughter's feet disappeared, Julie followed, but not before she heard Wife's answer.

"Slow, Husband. Slow."

She landed beside Natty. The cedar basket followed but Julie didn't pause to wonder why it hadn't stayed in Yani's world. All she cared about was Natty was home. They took a moment to drink in the sight of each other. Then Julie wrapped her arms around Natalie Jade, kissed the top of her head, and snuggled. Together they lay on the forest floor until the first birds began to sing in the dawn.

* * *

Natty's return frustrated the police. Since they couldn't tell the cops what really happened, Julie fabricated a story for Natty to give them but made her swear she knew lying was wrong and wouldn't do it again. After promising, Natty told them she had escaped the kidnapper by jumping out of the truck when he stopped to pee. That she had run into the forest, gotten lost and in her confused wandering ended up at the cliff near her home. No, she didn't get a look at him. He wore a mask all the time. No, she didn't know where the other girls were. No, she didn't know where he was taking her. The story would fall apart under close scrutiny, but Natty made them believe her.

Julie, on the other hand, had a more difficult time. The police pushed and pushed, especially with their questions about Colby. Thank God, no one had seen her going into his place. They assumed Colby had been like his dad and had killed himself when Natty escaped. It hurt and bothered Julie for Colby's name to be tarnished like his dad's, but she couldn't do anything to change their minds. The cops even found the video of Yani, but they chalked it up to a disturbed mind trying to place blame elsewhere. Eventually, the police concluded that Natty was one very brave, and very lucky, little girl.

With the fact of Colby's death came the realization the other little girls were lost forever. The town began to mourn.

* * *

After the excitement and hubbub of Natty's return died down, mother and daughter stood together on the cliff, waiting for the right moment to say goodbye to Yani.

Lost in thought, Julie listened to the pounding waves. For the first time in a long while, she felt unsure about who she really was—her identity had been wrapped up in the past. Now here was the opportunity to discover what type of person she could be instead of running from herself, instead of becoming what others told her she was and wanted her to be. It offered a fresh start for her and her daughter and, in time, maybe she'd be share portions of her childhood with Natty. It might help her understand she wasn't alone. *Never too late, right?*

"Are you ready, sweetie?" Julie said.

"Yuppers."

Together they lit a match and bent to touch the cedar basket with the flame. It went up with a whoosh. The wood they set the basket on caught fire, and, when a knot popped, a shower of sparks spiraled into the air. As the flames licked the basket, none of the pyrotechnics Julie expected appeared, but within the curling smoke, the ghost of Yani looked at them. Julie watched until the red embers of Yani's eyes winked out.

Natty slipped her hand into Julie's. She looked down, and they smiled at each other. Nothing more needed to be said.

Hand in hand, they watched Yani's basket burn.

The End

Chris Marrs lives on the West Coast of British Columbia. She tends bar during the day to keep her kids fed, watered, and sheltered and spends the nights writing, usually accompanied by copious amounts of coffee and sometimes a little wine. She has a story in *A Darke Phantastique,* Cycatrix Press, *The Library of the Dead,* Written Backwards Press, and in *Dark Discoveries Issue #25/Femme Fatale, October 2013*. Bad Moon Books published her novella *Everything Leads Back to Alice* in the Fall of 2013. You can find her on Facebook where she "likes" more than posts or on Twitter.

www.ingramcontent.com/pod-product-compliance
Lightning Source LLC
LaVergne TN
LVHW091053080826
845145LV00002B/736